THE WORLDS GUARDSMEN

WE, THE PROTECTORS OF THE PEOPLE

BY

RODNEY P DAVIS

Published by Book Writing Pioneer

Cover design by Book Writing Pioneer

ISBN: Printed in the United States

BOOK WRITING
PIONEER

Table of Contents

◆◆◆

CHAPTER 1

THE BEGINNING

It was March 1898 in Portugal. At the age of eighteen, Lizzes Harriet and her boyfriend, Earl Melvin, decided to leave Portugal and migrate to England. Even though she was black, her light skin often led others to mistake her for white. Her boyfriend was a black man who was also light-skinned. When they arrived in England, she got a job the same day as a seamstress in a store called Royal Clothing. She was very good at her job as she was taught how to sew at a very young age in Portugal. No doubt, she was hired because of her beauty; she was a beautiful woman who spoke Portuguese and English. It was a little difficult for Earl to find a job, but he eventually secured a job as a cook at a restaurant called 'Courts of England.' They both lived together in a hotel, Brittles Hotel. They stayed there for two years until they saved up enough money to get their own home.

In January 1900, they decided to get married, and she became Mrs. Lizzes Melvin. In October of the same year, they had a daughter named Lizzie Melvin. Life was great and was about to get better. One day, the Queen of England visited the Royal Clothing Store to see who was in charge of making her dress for the upcoming baptism of her grandson. Nobody in the store wanted to take on that assignment due to the pressure that came with it. The store manager decided to give it to Lizzes because she was the best seamstress in the store. Lizzes worked day and night for three weeks, both at the store and at home, until November 22nd, 1900. She made the most elegant dress the store had ever produced.

The General store manager was so amazed by the dress that she tried to take credit for the design. When she personally delivered the dress, she told the Queen that she decided to make the dress herself after assigning it to Lizzes. But the Queen already knew who made the dress because her butler and Earl were very good friends. The butler had been to their home and seen Lizzes working on the dress with his own eyes. The Queen called the butler into her study and asked him who made the dress. The butler told her that Lizzes Melvin made the dress, not the store manager. What the General store manager didn't know was that her butler was reporting the progress of her dress to her daily. The Queen asked the General store manager again, "Who made the dress?" And she finally confessed that she lied about making the dress. The Queen informed the store owner about the incident, and the General store manager was suspended for two weeks without pay.

◆◆◆

CHAPTER 2

A NEW HOME

December 11th, 1900. At the Queen's grandson's baptism, she received so many compliments on her dress that it was becoming a little overwhelming. Everyone was amazed. Upon returning home, the Queen told her butler that she wanted to personally meet Lizzes at the castle to thank her for making the Queen's dress. The butler then went to Lizzes and Earl's home to inform her about the news. After receiving the news, Lizzes fainted with excitement! After waking up, she initially thought it was a dream but realized it wasn't when she saw the butler sitting on the couch. The butler asked her if she, Earl, and the baby would be able to accompany him to the Queen's home the next day at 10 am. Lizzes said yes with Earl's approval of the invitation. Lizzes told the butler to hold on for a minute, as they would have to inform their managers at work of what was about to take place so they wouldn't get in any trouble. What they didn't know was that the

Queen had already informed their managers that Lizzes and Earl would not be at work the next day due to their visit to her. The next day, the Royal Guard escorted Lizzes and Earl to the Queen's home. It was very exciting for them to be visiting the Queen. After entering the palace, they met the Queen in her living quarters.

The Queen welcomed Lizzes, Earl, and baby Lizzie with open arms. After they sat down, the Queen asked if baby Lizzie could be introduced to her grandson since they were the same age? Lizzes replied, "It would be an honor." The Queen called in the King, the Prince, the Princess, and her grandson. The King, the Prince, and the Princess were excited to meet the woman who made the Queen's dress, especially the Princess, since she had an upcoming event on February 22nd, 1901. The two babies were taken to the nursery where they were being tended to by the Princess nannies. The Queen asked Lizzes what she was thinking when she made her dress because it was extremely beautiful. Lizzes explained to her that she was inspired by the memories of her mother and her family back home, how they would go to the forest and look at all the beautiful aspects of the forest: the flowers, the different types of trees, the animals and how her family would just spend all day enjoying and thinking how beautiful nature was and that's where she got her inspiration for the dress design. The Queen and Princess were very impressed. But the men were not that much interested in dresses. So, the King asked Earl if he would like to see the kitchen since he was a great cook.

The Prince also joined them in the kitchen tour as he didn't want to hear any more 'dress talk.' After the men left the room, the Princess asked Lizzes if she could make a dress for her upcoming ball. Lizzes said, of course, but that would have to be relayed to her manager as all the sales had to be processed through the company. The Queen added that she would also need another dress for the Princess event. Lizzes replied, "That would take a good two months," but she was unsure if she would have that type of time with her and Earl working, the baby, and household needs. The Queen then made a suggestion and said to Lizzes, "Why don't you quit your job and move into the palace and become the Royal Family's personal seamstress?" Lizzes was stunned! She hadn't expected any of this. Lizzes asked, "Is this for real?" The Queen laughed and replied, "Of course." Lizzes asked, "What about Earl and his job?" The Queen and Princess laughed, saying, "Earl can have the job as a cook in the kitchen if he likes, and we wouldn't even think about having you here without your husband." The men returned to the room, and Earl noticed the stunned look on Lizzes' face. The Queen asked Earl, "Would you and your family like to move into the palace? You could have a job as a cook in our kitchen and Lizzes can be our personal seamstress, and baby Lizzie will have around-the-clock care." Earl looked at the King and Prince, who were nodding their head as if they were saying, “Yes.” Overwhelmed, Earl fainted.

CHAPTER 3

THE TRUTH SHALL SET YOU FREE.

After leaving the palace and returning home, Lizzes and Earl had a lot to talk about. First, Lizzes is thinking about how she's going to tell her manager that she's leaving to work at the palace as the Queen's personal seamstress. Earl is also thinking about how to break the news to his boss, as the Queen wanted the move to take place by the end of the week, and it was already Tuesday. Lizzes and Earl are worried that their friends, work friends, and those outside, will act differently towards them. Earl is more worried about something more serious than their work issues.

They have to tell the Queen that they are of black descent. Lizzes and Earl decided they would inform the butler to tell the Queen of their black descent before they quit their jobs since everyone thinks they're not black. The next morning, Earl meets the butler for coffee, as they do every morning before going to work. Earl shared the truth with the butler. He tells him that He and Lizzes are actually black, and they both have black fathers who married white women in Portugal. That's why their skin is so light. The butler wasn't shocked or even stunned. He knew they were of black descent but never said anything about it to them. But, the butler advised them to tell the Queen and the Royal Family before they moved into the palace. The butler assured them that it wouldn't make a difference, but it was important to tell them before someone else did. Before leaving, the butler said he would arrange a meeting with the Queen and let the Queen know that they had something to tell her. Now, Lizzes and Earl are both nervous and scared.

The next morning, Michael, the butler, came to escort Lizzes and Earl to the palace. He informs them to be honest and let whatever happens just happen. As soon as they reached the palace, the Queen awaited them in the front lobby. She seemed worried that Earl and Lizzes had changed their mind. Earl decided to be the man and speak first. As he told the Queen the news, they could tell the Queen was getting upset. The Queen stopped Earl and said, "I can tell you were not white. As you can see, we have lots of black people working in and outside of the palace. Michael, my butler, also works here and lives here." The Queen informed them that the family was excited to have them here and hoped that they hadn't changed their mind. Earl and Lizzes were both relieved and assured the Queen they would be happy to live and work in the palace. The Queen was excited. She showed them to their living quarters. It had three bedrooms with two full baths and a living room on the south end of the palace. She then introduced them both to the entire staff. Lizzes and Earl were relieved but realized they needed to inform their bosses and friends, both at work and outside, that they were moving into the palace and would be leaving their jobs at the end of the week.

◆◆◆

CHAPTER 4

FAMILY, FRIENDS, AND JEALOUSY

After leaving the palace and dropping the baby off at the nanny's, Lizzes and Earl decided to disclose the news to their bosses, one at a time. They also wrote a letter in Portuguese to inform their families back in Portugal about the change. Earl and Lizzes stopped at Earl's workplace first. First, Earl informed his boss that he would not be returning to work as he got a job inside the palace. He didn't mention that they would also be living in the palace since it wasn't necessary. Earl's boss was genuinely happy for him as he could find another good cook anywhere and told him not to be a stranger. He wished him the best, as did all of his former co-workers. For Lizzes, it was a different story. Lizzes and Earl went to Lizzes' place of work. Lizzes began to tell her manager that she would not be returning to work, as she would be working for the Queen as her personal seamstress. Lizzes' manager got really upset, telling her that she wouldn't last long there and would be back. She also said that she wouldn't hire her back even when she came running back. She went on to tell her that she wasn't welcome anymore at their private and personal women's events and clubs since the store manager was the president of most of the women's events and clubs. She also told her that she wasn't that good, just good enough to have kept a job there.

Lizzes was visibly upset upon hearing all of this. Earl stepped in, telling the manager, "After all of that you just said to Lizzes, she is the one who has a job in the palace, and you don't, and that's the only reason why you are upset because it's her and not you." Lizzes stops Earl and says, "Thank you for the opportunity to work here. I'm most grateful for the experience and the time spent here making friends. I hope that the friendships I've made here will continue since the move to the palace will not change me, nor will it break me. To you who want to continue being my friend, I will be at the coffee shop after work, same time as usual." Lizzes and Earl then left and headed to the coffee shop. They stayed there for about an hour. After some time, three guys showed up at the coffee shop and confronted Earl. One of the gentlemen said Earl cussed out his wife and threatened her. Earl said, "I didn't know such a thing."

As the guys approached Earl, they told him to take his wife and baby and leave the town immediately. Then, they left. The butler was sitting there with them. He advised Earl and Lizzes that it was unsafe for them to go home and suggested they go with him to the palace. Earl and Lizzes decided to take the butler's advice; they picked up baby Lizzie and headed to the palace. Earl, Lizzes, and the butler informed the Queen about what happened, but the Queen wasn't surprised. She knew something like this would happen because of jealousy. The Queen instructed Earl and Lizzes to stay in their quarters and told them that they could go tomorrow to retrieve their belongings from their home. They next morning, Lizzes and Earl were surprised to have their own Royal body guards!!

◆◆◆

CHAPTER 5

RESPECT THE GUARD

As Lizzes and Earl leave the palace and head to their home to retrieve their belongings, they are accompanied by four Royal Guardsmen dressed in royal suits that stand out and, according to Lizzes, are very loud. Lizzes had an idea for the guardsmen's uniform but she would have to ask the Queen first. As they approach the coffee shop, they see some of their former co-workers. Earl and Lizzes had no idea what to expect as they were being seen accompanied by their own personal security. People stared and talked as they entered the coffee shop. They sat down at the table while the Royal Guardsmen stood around them, observing the area. Three of Lizzes' friends approached her, but the Royal Guardsmen stopped them. Earl let the guardsmen know that it's ok, for they are their friends. As the three ladies sat down, they were confused about the guardsmen. Lizzes explained to them what happened at the coffee shop yesterday and that the Queen had decided to provide them with security. The ladies were stunned! Lizzes also explained that the Royal clothing store would no longer be making the Royal Family's clothing; instead, she would be doing that but would need a team. The ladies were excited and offered their services, thinking to themselves if Lizzes could get them a job with her at the palace. Lizzes said she would talk to the Queen later this evening. She also informed the three ladies that they were making a work area on the palace's second floor in the west wing, although she hadn't seen it yet. Lizzes asked the ladies as they got up to leave for work, not to mention anything to anyone until she had spoken with the Queen.

Earl and Lizzes departed from the coffee shop and headed to their home. Upon arrival, they found that their home had been vandalized. All their windows were broken, but before they could make another move, the guardsmen jumped into action. Two entered the house with guns drawn while the other two surrounded Earl and Lizzes. The two guardsmen who entered the house came out and reported that everything was clear and that whoever did this just broke the windows. Earl and Lizzes entered the house to find everything was intact, but the guardsmen escorted them out. Two guardsmen stayed behind while the other two took Earl and Lizzes back to the palace. The guardsmen informed the Queen of the situation and told her it wasn't safe for Earl and Lizzes to retrieve their belongings, so they would go back and do it themselves. The

Queen agreed and sent five more Royal Guardsmen to retrieve Earl and Lizzes' belongings. She also wanted the guardsmen to start their personal investigation outside of law enforcement and find out who vandalized Earl and Lizzes' property.

The Queen noticed that Lizzes was visibly upset, so she comforted her. She said, "Don't worry, this was expected. Some people are jealous and have a lot of hatred towards others who have been blessed with a gift by God." The Queen continued telling Lizzes, "You have a special gift. Don't let anyone stop or discourage you from using it. When you use the gift that God has given you, expect the unexpected." Lizzes answered, "Thank you! I really needed to hear that." Then she asked to speak with Earl in private as she was a wise Queen and had seen anger at its highest level before, and she is seeing it right now in Earl. She told Earl, "I've seen that anger before with my nephew, and nothing good is going to come out of it. Do not disgrace your family and this palace by taking revenge on something already being taken care of." Earl responded, "But your majesty, they threatened the lives of my family," and Earl began to cry! The Queen comforted Earl by saying, "I know they did, but I need you to trust me and let the guardsmen do their job. Now, go and comfort your family. They need you right now." Earl agrees, saying, "Thank you, Your Majesty," and goes back to his family.

Earl and Lizzes headed back to their quarters to rest, but Lizzes remembered that she needed to talk to the Queen and asked the Queen's guard if she could talk with the Queen. The guardsmen returned and said, "Yes, she will see you now." Lizzes began to discuss with the Queen about their personal guardsmen uniforms and asked if she could design something a little less formal for them to wear so they could blend in the crowd. The Queen said, "Yes, that's an excellent idea." Lizzes then asked if it would be ok to hire three of her former co-workers to help once the work area is completed. The Queen smiled and said, "Three! I think you're going to need more than that." Lizzes had a stunned look on her face. The Queen said, "Come with me." The Queen took Lizzes into the newly constructed work area. It had six work areas and everything Lizzes needed, including her own work area. Lizzes was stunned. The Queen smiled and said, "Walk around, get yourself acquainted." Lizzes asked, "When will it be ready?" The Queen replied, "In two weeks, on December 26th, after Christmas, it will be fully functional." The Queen departed, and Lizzes let out a huge scream and began to yell with excitement. The Queen paused for a minute to listen to Lizzes scream and yell! She then smiled and walked away.

CHAPTER 6

UNDERCOVER GUARDSMEN

As the guardsmen begin their investigation and the moving process of Earl and Lizzes' home, they uncover several significant clues. They discovered that the rocks thrown through the windows were a certain type that you can only get from a certain part of town. They also discovered that the store manager, her husband, and their two cousins lived in that part of town. However, they needed more proof. The guardsmen couldn't believe that the store manager's husband and two cousins, who had made a statement about Lizzes and Earl at the coffee shop, would actually commit the crime themselves. It seemed too easy. Therefore, the guardsmen examined the rocks more carefully and discovered that the weight of the rocks was very light and there were lots of them. They also discovered wheel tracks that looked like they were brushed away with a branch to hide the tracks. So, they started asking themselves: if I was going to throw a rock through a window, would it be a good size rock? Would there be lots of small ones? As they were moving boxes out of the house, one of the guardsmen noticed footprints, smaller ones than before.

The guardsmen put two and two together. They came up with the conclusion that the store manager, who also had a verbal confrontation with Lizzes, had something to do with it, but what part did she play? The guardsmen brought Lizzes and Earl's belongings to the palace. Then, they informed the Queen of the evidence that they found. The Queen instructed the guardsmen to continue investigating cause there had to be more behind the vandalism. The guardsmen set up a plan to catch the vandals red-handed. They believed if the vandals had done it once, they would do it again. The guardsmen replaced all the windows in Lizzes and Earl's home. They set two guardsmen who positioned themselves in the alley across the street to watch the house from a distance. The guardsmen paid a couple of spies to go into bars, take credit for the vandalism, and had other spies hype up the others claiming to take credit for the vandalism. The spies also noted that all the windows had been replaced and said they would go and break those windows as well. As the spies are being praised for the vandalism, two ladies walk out of the bar. The guardsmen spies noticed them. The two ladies entered another bar and joined two more ladies. The ladies began walking towards a home about four blocks away. The ladies walked into the house. After about ten minutes, the guardsmen couldn't believe their eyes. They were in disbelief at what they were seeing. On the porch, the ladies were talking to four kids. Three of the ladies were Lizzes' former co-workers and close friends whom she had met for coffee and thought about hiring, and the four kids couldn't be older than 13 or 14. It was nighttime; the kids left the porch and walked towards Earl and Lizzes' house with a wheel barrel full of rocks.

When they arrived at Earl and Lizzes' house with the wheel barrel full of rocks, the guardsmen showed up. The kids were scared to death because they knew who the guardsmen worked for: The Queen!!! The guardsmen escorted the kids back to the palace to confess to the Queen. The kids were sitting in the Queen's study. When she walked in, they were immediately overwhelmed with fear and regret. The Queen began to ask them why and who was involved in the vandalism. All the kids started talking at once, telling the Queen what had happened at the same time. The Queen clapped her hands and shouted, "Quiet!!!!" She picked out a young lady from the group and asked her, "Tell me, who told you young people to vandalize the home?"

The young lady gave the three mothers and the store manager's name, who all worked at the Royal Clothing Store. One of the guardsmen told the Queen that he thinks Lizzes is going to hire these three ladies to work with her in the palace. The Queen was visibly upset. She asked, “What type of people would use their children to commit a crime?”

CHAPTER 7

JURISDICTION AND JUSTIFICATION

The Queen instructed the guardsman to escort the kids back home and tell the ladies that the kids were caught red-handed and had confessed, and she would let Lizzes and Earl decide their fate. The Queen called Earl and Lizzes into her study and began to tell them what had happened. Lizzes was shocked to find out that her three close friends were involved and even more disturbed to learn that they used their kids to do their dirty work. Lizzes and these ladies were very close, almost like sisters, so she was extremely distraught and in disbelief. But Earl, not so much. He knew the ladies were up to no good but didn't want to interfere with Lizzes' work. He had disagreed with Lizzes at the coffee shop when she offered to get them a job at the palace. When the guardsmen reached each kid's home, they relayed the Queen's message to each of the ladies. None of them said a word but stood there frightened to death cause this was the Queen they were dealing with, not the police.

The four ladies didn't know what to think because Lizzes had their fate in her hands, and they were thinking the worst since they had lied and were going to sabotage her job and relationship with the Queen. The four ladies decided that they would have a better chance with the police and chose to turn themselves in to save their kid's future. The four ladies gathered together and made their way to the police station. One of the ladies asked the officer on duty if they were conducting an investigation into the home that was vandalized. The officer responded, "Yes! But with no leads yet." They began to tell the police officer what happened. That's when the officer learned that the guardsmen were the ones who conducted their own investigation and the Queen was involved. The officer said, "Oh, I get it. Your fate is in the hands of the homeowner you vandalized per the Queen, and you thought you would get a slap on the wrist from the police." He continued, "The Queen doesn't get involved in police matters, but when she does, we have no jurisdiction over her and her decisions. Now, if you want me to lock someone up, why don't you tell those no-good husbands of yours who are always causing trouble to go commit a crime, and I would gladly lock them up." The ladies left the police station visibly upset and scared to death. Now, the three ladies whom Lizzes was going to hire turned against the store manager cause she was the reason all this happened. They realized what they had lost and could still lose. Now, they would have to wait on Lizzes to see what their fate would be. As the ladies walked away from the store manager, they passed by the town church and decided to walk in. There, they saw the bishop and began to tell him what happened. The bishop asked, "Would you like to be forgiven by God for your actions?" They responded, "Yes." He had them say a prayer. And then he said, "It's in God's hands now, and he has forgiven you." The ladies left the church and went home.

The next morning, Lizzes showed up at the coffee shop as usual with her guardsmen, this time without Earl, as did the three ladies. Lizzes and the ladies made eye contact. Lizzes could see that they were not themselves and that they had this look of shame on their faces. One of the ladies decided to go over, apologize to Lizzes, and confess. As she got up and walked towards Lizzes, the guardsmen asked to search her and her belongings in front of everyone. After the search, the lady sat down with shame in her eyes. Then the other ladies came over and also sat down with shame in their eyes. One of the ladies said, "We know what we did was wrong. We lied and had sabotage in our hearts, and betrayed our friendships because of jealousy. We got our kids involved, and we are very ashamed. We know our punishment for our actions is in your hands, and we gladly accept it without hesitation. We just ask that our kids be left out of it. We put them up to it, and they're just kids."

One of the ladies said, "We also quit our jobs at the Royal Clothing store." Lizzes stopped them as she was visibly crying. One of the guardsmen asked Lizzes, "Is everything ok?" She said, "Yes!" Lizzes said, "You ladies really hurt me, but I must forgive you. But kids!!!! You ladies used your kids!!" One of the ladies began to say, "Yes, we know it was stupid; we weren't thinking, and jealousy and anger got the best of us." Lizzes went on to say, "It's deeper than that. Any woman who would use her kids to do a crime is either really messed up emotionally or was forced to do it. But we won't get into that right now, but I won't forget it either." She continued, asking the ladies, "Since your fate is in my hands, would you like to know what it is?" The ladies all replied, "Yes!" Lizzes said, "Come with me."

CHAPTER 8

DOING THE UNTHINKABLE

As Lizzes and the women exited the coffee shop, the ladies were visibly nervous. They wondered what could be on Lizzes' mind. They would not have to wonder anymore as the ladies were chatting amongst themselves in their own horse and carriage; they followed Lizzes and her closely trailing guardsmen. The ladies, who were not paying attention, suddenly realized they were heading to the palace. The ladies' nervousness escalated into animated horror. They couldn't believe Lizzes had brought them to the palace. The three ladies were so horrified that they tried to jump out and run, but the guardsmen stopped them, and Lizzes confronted the ladies. The ladies confessed to Lizzes that they couldn't face the Queen! "There is no way we can do that," they insisted. Lizzes responded, "It's either this or jail," she added, "And I really don't want to put you in jail and take you away from your kids." The ladies began to beg Lizzes, "Please, anything but this." Lizzes remarked, "It's this or jail, and please don't make me do that." Lizzes continued, "You had the courage to put your kids' lives in jeopardy. You had the courage to get me to hire you so you can sabotage my life and relationship with the Queen, but you don't have the courage to face the Queen?" The ladies began to reflect on everything Lizzes had said and decided to go with Lizzes inside the palace.

Now, the Queen has no idea that Lizzes has brought these ladies to the palace, and Lizzes has no idea how the Queen will react. Lizzes is also nervous, but she isn't showing it. Lizzes and the ladies entered the palace. Lizzes directed the ladies to follow her into her study quarters. The ladies were stunned by the beauty of the palace and Lizzes' living quarters. She instructed the ladies to wait here. She first went to get Earl and brought him into the study where the ladies were. Earl was shocked but not angry. He looked at his wife and declared, "I don't know what you're thinking or what you're up to, but you're my wife, so I'm going to trust your decisions." He also added, "I am staying out of this," He told the ladies to have a good day and walked out. Lizzes felt slightly relieved because she thought he would be angry and disgusted at the ladies, but he wasn't. Now came the hardest part. Lizzes told the ladies she would be right back. Lizzes went to fetch the Queen. The Queen walked in, saw the ladies, and exploded in anger! She condemned the ladies for what they did. She declared that they should be locked up and the key would be thrown away for what they put those kids through. She asked, "What kind of parents are you!??" One of the guardsmen had a smile on his face as if wanting to say, *"Like yeah, get them."* The Queen noticed the guardsman smiling, and he immediately erased that smile as she gave him a look from hell!! The Queen demanded the ladies to explain themselves. After hearing the ladies' explanation and seeing how shameful, hurt, embarrassed, and upset they were, she turned and asked Lizzes, "Well, what do you want to do with these ladies?" Lizzes responded to the Queen, "I want to hire them to work with me." The ladies were completely stunned! As was the Queen.

The Queen stared at Lizzes for about ten seconds as Lizzes lowered her head, not wanting to meet the Queen's eye. The Queen commanded, "Look at me," Lizzes looked up at the Queen. The Queen declared, "If this is their fate, then so be it. I trust you know what you are doing." Then the Queen turned to the ladies and remarked, "You should thank God for this young lady. She could have put you in jail out of anger and revenge, but she chose to forgive you and hire you out of love and compassion." Then the Queen told the ladies, "You now have a second chance. I promise you; you will not get a third." The Queen bid the ladies good day and walked out. Lizzes was totally relieved because she didn't know how this would unfold, and the ladies could see how relieved she was. One of the ladies inquired to Lizzes, "You didn't have a clue of how this was going to play out, did you?" Lizzes admitted, "No, I didn't." Another lady asked, "You risked your life and livelihood for us? Why?" Lizzes responded, "I have seen how afraid your kids were when they confessed. Also, the kids were visibly concerned about you, wondering if their mothers were going to jail and what would happen to them if you ladies did go to jail." She continued, "I just couldn't do that to those kids. So, I did the unthinkable. I choose to make sure those kids have a future by hiring you because if I didn't, I believe you would go crawling back to the Royal Clothing store asking for your jobs back and being under the control of an evil person." One of the ladies questioned, "Speaking of the store manager, what will her fate be?" Lizzes smiled and replied, "I'm glad you asked," as she glanced at her guardsmen.

CHAPTER 9

CHANGING OF THE GUARDSMEN

As Lizzes escorted the ladies out of the palace, they left with a sense of happiness and excitement. However, they were very curious about the fate of the store manager. As each lady reached home, they shared the good news with their kids. The ladies could see the relief on their kid's faces. But their husbands were visibly upset because they blamed the ladies for the kids getting caught. The next day, the ladies had a meeting at the coffee shop before Lizzes arrived. They decided it was time for their husbands to leave but wanted to discuss with Lizzes how to handle this because their husbands were verbally and sometimes physically abusive. They know they need to get away from them, as they are a bad influence on their kids. Lizzes and Earl finally arrived at the coffee shop. The three ladies approached to greet Lizzes and Earl. They began to discuss their husbands with Lizzes and sought her advice. Lizzes and Earl agreed with the ladies that their husbands' bad reputation in town and with the police must be dealt with before they do any more damage.

Lizzes announced she had an idea. She asked the three ladies, "If this is what you want?" The ladies immediately replied, "Yes," Lizzes responded, "Ok." But one of the ladies questioned, "It was our husbands' idea to vandalize your home and try to run you out of town. Why come they are not in trouble with the Queen?" Lizzes assured, "They are! I didn't tell you, ladies, but your kids said it was their dad's idea to vandalize our home in the first place, and their fate was also in our hands, as per the Queen. Your husbands have caused so much trouble in the past that I don't think the Queen really cares about them that much. I was just going to have them locked up, but only after your fate was decided. But I have a better idea." She conveyed her plan to one of the guardsmen. The guardsmen looked at Lizzes and remarked, "Perfect." Lizzes then informed the ladies, "It's done." The ladies asked, "What's done." Lizzes proclaimed, "Your husbands will be gone before you get home." The ladies were shocked to hear that. Lizzes urged, "Trust me." The two guardsmen departed, while two stayed with Lizzes, Earl, and the three ladies. After about two hours, the guardsmen returned and confirmed to Lizzes, "It's done." Lizzes reassured the ladies, "It's done! Your husbands will not verbally or physically abuse you ever again."

The ladies asked Lizzes, "What happened?!!" Lizzes replied, "I will tell you later, but we have to go to the Royal Clothing Store." The ladies were curious about what was going to happen at the Royal Clothing Store. As Lizzes, Earl, the ladies, and the guardsmen left the coffee shop, they noticed a horse and carriage, accompanied by four other guardsmen, leaving town. One of the ladies spotted a gentleman staring at them as they were leaving. The ladies exchanged looks at each other, murmuring, "They look like our husbands." The ladies inquired, "Were those our husbands leaving town with four guardsmen?" Lizzes assured them, "Trust me, it's for the good. I will tell you later." The ladies were so confused but trusted Lizzes. As the horse and carriage disappeared into the distance, Lizzes, Earl, and the three ladies made their way to the Royal Clothing Store.

As they entered the store, the store manager appeared visibly concerned. She knew Lizzes was there to deliver her fate. The store manager had been dreading this day for a week. Lizzes instructed Earl and the ladies to stay put. She signaled the guardsmen to follow her. One of the ladies asked Earl, "What is she going to do?" Earl responded, "The Hell if I know." Lizzes approached the store manager and clarified, "I didn't come here to chastise you or seek revenge. I am letting you know that your husband will not be home when you get there, as he is a bad influence on you and the kids." She then began to tell the store manager, "I have a different plan for you. Given all of your anger, evilness, and disrespectful nature, you will become the first female guardsman. You need to learn respect and discipline for your kids. You will be leaving and starting your training in one week on December 26th, the day after Christmas. That is your fate." Earl, the ladies, and the store employees were stunned!! The store manager shot back, "What is my alternative?" Lizzes replied, "Jail." The store manager then asked, "What about my kids? And how long is this training?" Lizzes explained, "Your two kids will stay with one of the ladies, and the training is twelve weeks long. After the training, you will become my first female guardsman. You will return home after twelve weeks, and further training will continue for the next five years."

Lizzes continued, "It's either this or jail. It's your choice." The store manager responded, "I accept." Lizzes replied, "Ok. And have a good day." As Lizzes, Earl, and the ladies leave the Royal Clothing Store. Earl asked Lizzes, "Did you get this approved by the Queen?" Lizzes declared, "No. We are going to ask her tomorrow." Earl said, "Oh, no, not 'we'— 'you.' I don't want any part of this." Lizzes grinned at Earl, already knowing what he was going to say. Lizzes assured, "Don't worry, Earl, I'll tell her my idea and why. I'm pretty sure she will agree." Lizzes added, "I think."

CHAPTER 10

THE HIDDEN TRUTH

The next morning, Earl woke up earlier than Lizzes. Gets dressed and heads to the coffee shop without Lizzes, as he is trying to get out of the palace before Lizzes can share her idea with the Queen. Lizzes got up to find Earl not there and realized that he left. Lizzes went down to the kitchen with baby Lizzie for breakfast. The Queen, King, Princess, and Prince, along with their son, had already arrived just before Lizzes. The Queen inquired, "Where is Earl?" Lizzes explained, "He got up early this morning and left for the coffee shop." Not really knowing where he went, Lizzes realized this was the best time to tell the Royal Family of her decisions and ideas. Lizzes addressed the Queen, "Your majesty, I have something to tell you." The King and Prince looked at each other, understanding why Earl wasn't at breakfast, which he never missed. The King and Prince decided it was time to get out of there, but the Queen stopped them. Lizzes informed the Queen, "I made a decision on the store manager's fate." The Queen agreed, "Yes, she really needs to either be locked up or have a doctor check her out because something isn't right with her," she then asked, "What did you decide?" Lizzes declared, "I'm sending her off to be trained as the first female guardsman. She needs to learn respect and discipline." The King shockingly remarked, "Female guardsmen?" Lizzes confirmed, "Yes, King." The King disputed, "There are thousands of men who could not pass that training. What makes you think a woman can pass it?" Lizzes asserted, "I have faith in her. She has a different type of strength." The King said, "I can guarantee she will not pass that training. It's impossible for a woman to do it." The Prince also sided with the King, adding, "The obstacles are almost impossible for a man, and some men have died of exhaustion." Lizzes persisted, "I have seen something in her." The King then posed, "What if she dies? The kids will not have a mother."The King continued, "Lizzes, you have had some good ideas, but this one is guaranteed to fail."

The King then looked at the Queen and stated, "I know you are not going to approve of this since you have seen with your own eyes what type of training those guardsmen go through." The Queen told Lizzes very calmly, "You are a very bright and intelligent young lady. Your ideas are outstanding, but you have no authority over the Royal Guardsmen and who becomes a Royal Guardsman. When it comes to the Royal Guardsmen, you bring those decisions to me and only me. Are we clear?" Lizzes responded, "Yes, Your Majesty." The Queen added, "But I'm very curious about how this idea of yours turns out." The King stood up and left the room, with the Prince following him, pleading, "Father, please just give it a chance." Lizzes looked at the Queen and questioned, "Does that mean you approve?" The Queen affirmed, "Yes." The Princess leaned over and whispered to Lizzes, "I love that idea." The King and Prince returned to the room. The Queen inquired to Lizzes, "So what did you decide to do with those ladies' husbands?" Lizzes looked at the Queen and revealed, "I sent them to work in the prison. They will work there for one year. Cleaning up bathrooms and prison cells and doing whatever tasks at the prison will be necessary to teach them some respect for women. They will live at the prison but not with the prisoners."

The Queen questioned, "How did the ladies take the news of their husbands going to work at the prison for one year?" Lizzes declared, "I didn't tell them. The ladies decided it was time for them to go, but I didn't tell the ladies where they were going." The King exclaimed, "You didn't tell them?" Lizzes disclosed, "No, King, sir." The King interrogated, "What prison did you send those men to work at?" Lizzes responded, "IronRock!!!" The King burst out, "IronRock?!!! You sent those men to the most dangerous prison in the country over vandalism??" The Queen intervened, commanding the guardsmen, "Move those men to the prison of solitude and downgrade their stay there to six months immediately!!" The Queen stated, "Those men won't last a week in IronRock." Lizzes asserted, "I told those ladies that they will never have to worry about their abusive husbands again." The King remarked, "You got that right 'cause they will be dead in a week." The Queen reflected, "What about the kids? Legally, you can't keep the men away from their kids once their task is done. That will be up to the ladies and the court." Lizzes understood and realized that she had gone too far. Just then, Earl walked in and asked, "Is everything is ok?" Lizzes answered, "Yes!" With a mad look on her face. The King noted, "I know that look—somebody's in trouble." Just then, the butler entered and announced, "The new work area is ready, my Queen."

CHAPTER 11

ALL WORK, NO PLAY

December 20th, 1900. The next morning, Earl awakened in the guest room just as the Prince walked down the hallway toward the kitchen for water. He approached Earl and teased, "I bet you won't sneak out of the palace and leave your wife again." Earl smiled and replied, "Not on your life." Earl went to the room where Lizzes and the baby were and found the door locked. He knocked on the door and pleaded, "Lizzes, can you please open up? I'm sorry!" Lizzes responded, "I'll see you at breakfast." Earl walked back to the guest room, got dressed, and went to have breakfast. The Queen and King were there, as well as the Prince and Princess with their son. Earl walked in, and the Queen quipped, "Huh!! How was the guest room?" And everyone began to laugh. Earl confessed, "I didn't sleep at all, and Lizzes won't let me in our room." The King chuckled, "Oh yeah! She's angry." Lizzes entered with the baby, and Earl hopped up to pull out her chair.

Lizzes greeted, “Thank you and good morning,” to the Royal Family. Earl began to apologize, but Lizzes immediately cut him off, stating, “Not here! Later!” Earl agreed, “Ok,” as the Royal Family all are glued to Lizzes and Earl, anticipating what would happen next. Lizzes informed the Queen, “I’m going to start working on the Princess’s dress today. Do you know exactly who else needs a dress besides you and the Princess?” The Prince interjected, “Excuse me, Your Majesty, but could Lizzes make me a nice suit for the Princess’s ball?” The Queen inquired, “Well, Lizzes, can you?” Lizzes replied confidently, “Sure, but while I’m at it, Queen, do you mind if I start designing a new uniform for the guardsmen you appointed to Earl and myself?”

The Queen agreed and said, “Yes.” Then Lizzes explained, “I would like for them to blend into the crowd just so for their safety and protection. Right now, everyone knows who they are and where they are just because they stand out.” The King suggested, “While you’re at it, design me a suit for the Princess’s ball.” Lizzes responded, “Ok, I’ll just design the Royal Family’s special clothing for the Princess’s ball.” After breakfast, Lizzes instructed one of her guardsmen to inform the three ladies that they would begin work today and should report to the palace in two hours. Lizzes asked the Queen, “After the ladies’ kids get out of school, do you mind if they come to the palace? I could really use their help, and their mothers would probably appreciate having them here?” The Queen consented, "Yes! But make sure they don't get caught walking around the palace without supervision." Lizzes expressed her gratitude, "Thank you, your majesty." She handed the baby to the nannies and hurried off to the new work area. Earl muttered, "I guess I will report to the kitchen early and start working," feeling somewhat less important.

As Lizzes was setting up the work area, the three ladies on their way to the palace, decided to stop by Darlene's house, the former store manager. They knocked on her door, and Darlene came out, immediately snapping, "What do you ladies want? As I remember, you left me at the police station, and I haven't heard or seen you since then." One of the ladies, Vivian, explained, "We wanted to check on you cause we know the task you have is almost impossible, and we wanted to just come to see you. We were worried about you." Darlene responded curtly, "I don't need you to worry about me; I will be fine." Another lady, Alicia, added gently, "We don't mean to upset you, but just to let you know, when you leave next week, we will take good care of your kids for the 12 weeks that you will be gone." Just then, Darlene began to cry! This was the first time any of the ladies had seen any emotion besides her anger and jealousy. Through her tears, Darlene confessed, "I don't think I can do this. My husband is gone, and I don't know if I can stay gone from my kids for 12 weeks. I'm just not emotionally ready for all this; it's just too much." Darlene continued, "The word has gotten out on what we have done and our punishment around town. They're saying I'm going to die doing the training and that no woman will ever pass those obstacles." Another one of the ladies, Josephine, chimed in, "Well, I guess you're going to have to prove them all wrong! You have to do this for all of us women! When you pass this training, you will be a hero to all of us," Josephine encouraged. Alicia affirmed, "Exactly!! Now, you need to get yourself mentally ready. Don't worry about anything here; we will take care of your kids and your home, and when you come back, we will have a big celebration as you will be a guardsman and a hero!"

Darlene wiped her tears away and declared, "You're right! I'll show them. I'll show all of them!" Vivian added excitedly, "Oh yeah, just to let you know, Lizzes is counting on you to pass this training! Don't let her down!" The ladies hugged Darlene and then left for the palace. Upon reaching the palace, the guardsmen led the ladies to the new work area and they were stunned with excitement. Seeing their startled faces, Lizzes inquired, "Well, how do you like it?" The ladies exclaimed, "It's amazing." Lizzes began to show them the workload that they already had. Lizzes informed the ladies, "You will be making 50 pounds per week, 8 hours a day." The ladies were shocked, as they had only made 47 pounds per month at the Royal clothing store. Lizzes announced, "Let's get started." Alicia hesitated, then asked, "Before we get started, can you answer a question for us?" Lizzes affirmed, "Sure." Alicia paused for a moment, then asked, "What did you do with our husbands?" Lizzes, with a sorrowful look, admitted, "To be honest with you ladies, I sent them to work in the prison for six months. They will eat and sleep for free. They are not prisoners themselves, but they will be cleaning up the prison 8 hours a day. Their salary will be given to them when they leave. Hopefully, this will teach them how to respect women when they return." Lizzes added, "I can't tell you, ladies, what to do with your husbands when they return; that will be up to you." The ladies had a relieved look on their faces and agreed, "Ok, let's get to work."

◆◆◆

CHAPTER 12

TROUBLE WHEN YOU LEAST EXPECT IT

The next morning, Earl awoke in the guest room, upset because Lizzes had not set up a time to talk yesterday and had ignored him after work. Earl left the palace without the guardsmen. Since it was his day off, he headed to the coffee shop. Lizzes got up and made her way to the dining room, passing by the guest room, but she didn't see Earl. She thought he would be at breakfast already. Upon arriving, she found the Royal Family already gathered. She sat down and greeted everyone with a "Good morning" and began to feed baby Lizzie. The Queen inquired, "How was your first day at work?" Lizzes beamed, "It was so much fun. We stopped working at 8 pm." Then the Queen asked, "Where is Earl?" Lizzes, with a worried look, replied, "I don't know." The Queen questioned, "Did he sleep in the guest room last night?"

Lizzes embarrasly said, “Yes!” The Queen looked visibly concerned. She asked Lizzes, “Have you talked to him? have you given him a chance to apologize?” Lizzes admitted, “No.” The Queen then added with an angry look on her face, “I’m going to tell you this, then I’m going to leave it alone. You found compassion in your heart to forgive those ladies who tried to do harm to you and your family, but you don’t have that same compassion to have a talk with your husband, to accept his apology and move on? You haven’t spoken to your husband in two days.” Lizzes was visibly upset and had her head down. The Queen asserted, “You are wrong, and you need to fix it!” The Queen glanced at Lizzes’ security and realized that they were all present. She questioned the guardsmen, “Why aren’t you with Earl?” The guardsmen explained, “He told us he wanted to be alone today.” The Queen gave Lizzes a piercing look, then stood up and said, “Have a good day.” The Princess reassured Lizzes, “Don’t worry, when he comes back, have a talk with him.” Lizzes nodded, rose, and headed to the work area.

At lunchtime, Lizzes and the ladies made their way to the dining area. She informed the ladies that she would meet them there. She checked the guest room, but Earl was not there. She went to their room, but no sign of Earl. She visited the study where Earl loves to read, but no Earl. She headed to the garden where she and Earl often spent time, yet Earl was nowhere to be seen. Growing increasingly concerned because this had never happened before, she didn't know what to do. She went and found the Princess in the dining area and whispered in her ear, "I can't find Earl anywhere." Noticing the concern on Lizzes' face, the Princess soothed her and said, "Calm down." Then, she summoned the guardsmen and instructed them to go find Earl as she calmed Lizzes down. The guardsmen departed from the palace. An hour later, they returned to the palace with Earl, who was unconscious. The guardsmen told the butler to get the palace doctor and nurse. They took Earl to the guest room, where they started to give him an I.V. The doctor said in disbelief, "My goodness, he reeks of alcohol." Then the Queen and King entered the room along with the Prince and Princess and asked, "What's wrong?" The doctor explained, "He's had a little too much to drink. He will be fine once the I.V. begins to work through his body, but for now, the nurse will watch over him until he comes to consciousness." The doctor added, "I will go and tell Lizzes. Thank God they found him when they did." The Queen stopped the doctor and asserted, "No, I will go and tell her!" She was resisting her anger to burst out. The Princess was crying in the Prince's arms; she turned and asked the guardsmen, "Where did you find him?" The guardsmen responded, "At their home, passed out on the couch." The Queen entered the work area, causing everyone to stop what they were doing. Lizzes sensed something was wrong. The Queen told Lizzes, "Earl is in the guest room; go to him." Lizzes nodded, "Ok." The Queen instructed the ladies to continue working and informed them that Lizzes would not be returning for the rest of the day.

Vivian inquired of the Queen, “Your majesty, is everything ok?” The Queen assured her, “Yes, everything is fine. We just have a family matter that needs Lizzes attention. She will return to work tomorrow.” The Queen continued, “For now, continue working, and I will send the Princess to check on you later. Have a good day, ladies.” Lizzes entered the guest room, saw Earl lying there with an I.V. in his arm, and began screaming hysterically. The Prince quickly grabbed her, holding her to calm her down. The Prince soothed her by saying, “He’s ok. He just had too much to drink. He is resting and will wake up pretty soon.” Lizzes calmed down and sat beside Earl. She began to say, “Earl, I’m sorry for the way I’ve been acting for these last two days. Please wake up.” She laid her head on the pillow beside Earl and continued talking to him. “This is my fault,” she whispered. “I’m sorry. Please come back to me, please!” Tears began to stream down her face. The Princess gestured for the nurse to give Lizzes and her husband some privacy. After about 40 minutes, Earl stirred and woke up, confused about what was going on. He looked at Lizzes and asked, “What happened?”She explained, “You drank too much and passed out.” Earl’s memory got cleared. He began to apologize, but Lizzes stopped him. “We will talk tomorrow; I just need you to rest now,” she insisted. Lizzes said, “I will be right back,” and stepped outside to fetch the nurse.

She informed the nurse, “Earl is awake.” The nurse came in and checked Earl’s vitals. “I’m going to leave the I.V. in for ten more minutes,” she stated. She then added, “I will be right outside the door,” before leaving.

Lizzes informed Earl, “I’m going to get the baby. I’ll be right back.” As Lizzes was leaving, she encountered the Queen, who was on her way to check on Earl. Lizzes updated the Queen, “Earl is awake.” The Queen responded, “Good, I’m going to go check on him.” Lizzes acknowledged, “Ok.” The Queen walked to Earl and asked, “Earl, how do you feel.” Earl replied, “A lot better.” The Queen nodded and said, “Good. You and I will meet in my private studies tomorrow morning.” She added, “Glad you’re feeling better,” then left. Lizzes returned to the room, and the nurse was taking out Earl’s I.V. She asked Earl, “What did the Queen say?” “She said she wanted to see me in her private study tomorrow,” Earl explained. Lizzes reassured him, “Well, let’s not worry about that right now, just rest for now.” Lizzes began to read to Earl and the baby until both drifted off to sleep.

◆◆◆

CHAPTER 13

THE QUEEN OF HEARTS

The next morning, Earl woke up with a severe headache. Lizzes woke up and offered, "Let me get you some water." When Lizzes returned, she found Earl throwing up in the bathroom toilet. Lizzes went to the bathroom and handed Earl a towel. Earl was feeling better since he'd thrown up. Lizzes gave Earl the water and instructed, "Brush your teeth before you come back to bed." Earl decided to take a bath. After his bath, he returned to bed and told Lizzes, "I'm going to skip breakfast today." Lizzes responded, "Ok, go back to sleep." Three hours later, there was a knock at the door; it was a guardsman. Lizzes got up, and the guardsmen relayed to Lizzes that the Queen wanted to see Earl in 30 minutes. Lizzes acknowledged, "Ok." Earl, having overheard the conversation, got up and dressed. The guardsman returned, knocked on the door, and announced, "The Queen will see you now." The guardsman escorted Earl to the Queen's study. She was there waiting for him. Earl entered the Queen's study, and the guardsman closed the door behind him. The Queen invited Earl, "Please have a seat." The Queen inquired, "Earl, how are you feeling?" Earl replied, "I have a headache, and I'm feeling sick, but I'll be ok." The Queen said, "Good!" The Queen explained, "The reason why I called you in this morning is because I want you to know that you scared us all yesterday. Especially your wife!" The Queen then asked, "Earl, what made you want to drink alcohol?" Earl admitted, "Lizzes was angry with me, and I felt left out of everything like I didn't matter at all." The Queen assured, "Well, you do matter, as you can see. Your wife was frightened to death when the guardsmen found you and brought you back. The Princess was crying, and I, along with the Prince and King, were very concerned. If the guardsmen had not found you, you probably wouldn't be here with us today. You were unconscious when they found you. You cannot do that ever again. You and Lizzes are part of this family now. You will make a promise to me right now that you will never do that again, and if you're having any problems or dangerous thoughts, you will talk to someone."

Earl vowed, "I promise you that I will never do that again." The Queen nodded, "Ok. Will I see you at breakfast?" Earl declined, "No, Your Majesty, I'm going to rest for the rest of the day." The Queen agreed, "A good idea. Go get some rest." Earl said, "Thank you," and then left. Earl returned to his room, where Lizzes was getting the baby ready for breakfast. She asked Earl, "How did your meeting with the Queen go?" Earl explained, "She was very concerned and made me promise her that I would not do that again cause I frightened everyone." Lizzes agreed, "Yes, you did." Earl apologized, "I'm sorry," and Lizzes reassured him, "All is forgiven, and if you do that again, you won't have to worry about the alcohol killing you, 'cause I will!" Lizzes added with a smile, "Get some rest. I'll come check on you during my lunch break." Earl replied, "Ok." He climbed back into the bed and wished Lizzes, "Have a nice day." At breakfast, the Queen asked Lizzes, "Is the family ok?" Lizzes knew exactly what the Queen meant and responded, "Yes, everything is ok."

The Queen smiled and said, "Good, I'm happy to hear that." The Queen inquired, "Lizzes, what is the store manager's name," to which Lizzes replied, "Darlene." The Queen informed, "Her training starts in two days. Have you talked to her?" Lizzes responded, "No, I haven't yet." The Queen suggested, "You should go and talk to her. Maybe give her…" The Queen stopped herself and continued, "Better yet, have one of your guardsmen stop by her house and give her some encouragement and motivation." Lizzes agreed, "Ok, I like that idea." Lizzes sent one of her guardsmen to encourage Darlene before her training began.

The guardsman arrived at Darlene's house and knocked on the door. He asked, "May I come in?" Darlene warmly responded, "Yes, of course." Her two kids were excited to see a guardsman in their home. Darlene instructed her kids, "Go to your room and close the door." The guardsman began, "This is from the Queen. As the first female guardsman you will make 100 pounds a week, that's 20 pounds more than all the male guardsmen. You will have jurisdiction over all police officers and all government officials across the land. You will be world-known across the globe, and you will personally be escorting The Royal Family on any and all journeys cause you will be unique in character. You will have the respect of all the people especially the men. But what I'm about to tell you is a secret, and you cannot tell anyone."

He then reveals, "Lizzes is training her own special guardsmen. They will be called the World Guardsmen. As a world guardsman, you will be required to have other special requirements that I won't get into right now, but I can tell you. You will be speaking at least six different languages. That's just one of the requirements of a world guardsmen. As of right now, Lizzes speaks three different languages and is learning three more. She is also writing her own language called Guardishian. Once the language is complete, she will teach it to her guardsmen. The world guardsman is still a couple of years away from being introduced, so you cannot say anything to anyone." Darlene acknowledged, "Ok." The guardsmen told Darlene, "A lot of people are depending on you to pass your training. So, that same energy you had when you were vandalizing, you need to transform into that person when you go to training. Be mean, be angry, be sneaky, be destructive. Use your manager skills. You do whatever you have to do to pass that training, are we clear?" Darlene affirmed, "Yes, I'm ready." The guardsman looked into her eyes and confirmed, "Yes, I can see that you are. I will be back tomorrow with the layout of your training," he added. "By the way, the Queen wanted me to inform you of your husband's whereabouts. He and the other three men are working at the Prison of Solitude for the next six months. They're not prisoners but will be living in separate quarters away from the prisoners until their time is up. This is their punishment for their part in the vandalism. Have a good day, madam." The guardsman concluded.

Darlene felt excited, special, and relieved by the news about her husband. She understood that she must pass this training by any means necessary and do it with more brain than muscles. Knowing that once she received the layout of her training, she would have to put a plan together in one day in order to pass it. The guardsmen returned to the palace. He found the Queen and reported, "She is ready, and she is about to shock all of England." The Queen replied, "Good! There is a reason Lizzes picked her for this training. There is something else happening here. I just don't know, but I'm going to let it play out. What I've learned about Lizzes since she's been in the palace is that she has a reason for everything she does." She then instructed, "Send someone to keep an eye on Darlene's safety when she leaves for her training. Make sure none of those men try anything 'cause men will be men." The guardsmen accepted, "Ok, Your Majesty," and then departed.

CHAPTER 14

THE HOUSE HAS SECRETS

During her lunch break, Lizzes went to check on Earl. It is no surprise to her to find him still asleep. She checked his vitals, but everything seemed normal. Earl woke up for a minute. Lizzes asked, "How are you feeling?" Earl replied, "I still have a slight headache, but I feel better." Lizzes encouraged Earl, "Sit up and try to eat some fruit that I brought from the kitchen." Earl began to eat the fruit and finished all of them. Lizzes smiled, "Good, you will feel better by the morning." She added, "I will see you after work this evening." Earl murmured, "Ok," and drifted back to sleep. At Darlene's house, the kids were becoming emotional, knowing their mother had only one day left before she headed off to her training. She reassured the kids, "When this is over, our lives will change, and people will look at us differently." Her oldest son, who is 14 years of age, asked, "Mom, why is all of this happening to us?" Darlene explained, "We did something wrong, and we got you guys involved. Your father will be back soon as he is working in the prison for the next six months." Her son questioned, "Is father a prisoner?" Darlene clarified, "No, son! Their punishment for their part in the vandalism is to work at the prison, not as a prisoner." She instructed her kids to prepare for dinner, but she couldn't get the thought out of her head about The World Guardsmen that Lizzes was organizing. She wondered, "Does Lizzes want me to be a part of it?" She wasn't sure.

Darlene felt more determined than ever to pass the training. After work, Lizzes arranged a meeting with the butler. She asked the butler tentatively, "Can I trust you?" The butler paused for ten seconds before responding, hinting at his hesitation. Then he finally said, "Yes," because he knew she had something going on in that 21-year-old brain of hers. She revealed to the butler, "There is a hidden door behind the dresser in Earl's and my room at our house."

"Starting tomorrow, every morning before you go to the coffee shop, I want you to take my writings to our house. Move the dresser, push open the secret door, and arrange the writings from bottom to top, from left to right, on the shelf in that secret room," she instructed methodically. She handed the butler her key to the house. She implored the butler, "Promise me you will not say anything to anyone, and you will not read my writings." The butler queried cautiously, "Does anyone else know about this agreement between us?" Lizzes asserted firmly, "No!" The butler pressed, "Not even Earl?" Lizzes confirmed with a hint of secrecy, "No! Not even the Queen." The butler, concerned, asked, "Is this something that's going to get you in trouble?" Lizzes smiled reassuringly and said, "No! This is going to make improvements in a lot of areas but I have to keep writings of my improvement somewhere safe so that I don't forget." The butler, puzzled, asked, "Why me? Why not one of your guardsmen?" Lizzes explained calmly, "No one will suspect you of anything, but the guardsmen stand out like a burning fire. Everyone is always watching them."

The butler remarked, "This must be very serious if you're not telling your husband." Lizzes replied and assured him, "Eventually, I will tell him, but only when my plans of improvement are in play." The butler nodded, "Ok." Lizzes responded with determination, "Great, I'll meet you in my study in the morning at 5." The next morning, Lizzes met the butler in her study and handed over her writings. The butler then left and headed towards Lizzes and Earl's house. Upon entering, he locked the door behind him. He found the dresser in the room, moved it, pressed the middle panel and the door to the secret room swung open. The room was enclosed with brick walls and had no windows, but it had vents in the top corners for air to flow in from the other rooms. The butler was amazed at the room's design. He did exactly what Lizzes instructed and exited the room. As he was about to leave the room, he heard footsteps. He dared not to move, fearing that whoever was in the house would catch him. He heard two familiar voices, and he knew those voices! It was two of Lizzes' guardsmen. He heard one of the guardsmen exclaiming, "I found Earl's watch." The butler prayed silently and said, "Please don't come into the room." One of the guardsmen mused, "I wonder if they are going to sell this house?" The other guardsmen countered, "Knowing Lizzes? No!" The guardsmen then departed.

The butler sneakingly exited the room and glanced out of the window, watching the two guardsmen disappear into the distance. The butler then left the house and made his way to the coffee shop. Thirty minutes later, Earl and Lizzes arrived. Lizzes wanted to get Earl out of the house for some fresh air. Earl mentioned that he was going to the bathroom, but he spotted the butler and went over to speak with him, then he headed to the bathroom. The butler approached and sat next to Lizzes and whispered, "Two of your guardsmen showed up at the house looking for Earl's watch when I was there." Lizzes speculated, "Earl must have told them yesterday to go look for his watch." The butler suggested carefully, "If we're going to do this, we also have to know what Earl is doing and if he talked to any Guardsmen concerning the house." Lizzes nodded in agreement. The butler then left the coffee shop and returned to the palace. Lizzes burst into laughter, imagining the look on the butler's face when the guardsmen showed up at the house. After finishing their coffee, Lizzes and Earl departed for the palace with their guardsmen.

◆◆◆

CHAPTER 15

THE STRENGTH OF A WOMAN

The decisive day had arrived for Darlene: December 26th, 1900, one day after spending Christmas with her kids. She was set to leave that morning to start her training. As she was gathering her things, she heard a knock at the door. It was Lizzes and the Princess. Darlene opened the door and was surprised. The Princess said, "No need for us to come in. We just wanted to stop by and pray with you before you leave and let you know that we women are counting on you." Lizzes explained earnestly, "This is the first of a lot of things that haven't been done and that will be done. But everything that hasn't been done and we want to be done depends on you passing this training." The Princess added gently, "We don't mean to put any more pressure on you, but we just wanted you to know how important this is." Lizzes reminded Darlene, "Remember how mean and angry you were when I told you I was leaving the Royal clothing store?" Darlene affirmed, "Yes!" Lizzes pressed, "I need you to be that person, do you understand?" Darlene confirmed resolutely, "Yes." The Princess inquired, "Are the kids still asleep?" Darlene responded, "Yes." Vivian was coming to pick them up at ten this morning. The Princess suggested, "Do you mind stepping outside so we can pray?" Darlene stepped outside; they held each other's hands, and the Princess began to pray.

After they prayed, Lizzes comforted Darlene, "No need to worry about any men trying anything. The Queen has ordered you to have security there around the clock. You will have your own sleeping quarters away from the men." Darlene felt so relieved to hear that. The Princess and Lizzes hugged Darlene, encouraging her to stay strong. As the Princess and Lizzes left, Darlene now realized that all the ideas that Lizzes wanted to put into effect depended on her passing the guardsmen training. At that moment, she felt something strange, like a strong presence around her. She experienced a sense of comfort and peace as she had a newfound energy. She finished her preparations and got her kids up and ready. Vivian knocked on the door; Darlene opened it to find Vivian stepping inside, tears streaming down her face. Darlene asked with concern, "Why are you crying?" Vivian sobbed, "You are getting ready to do something that, according to everyone in the town, is impossible for a woman. The people in the town are saying you are going to die during that training, and I'm scared for you." Darlene looked at Vivian firmly and said, "Look at me. Do I look nervous?

Do I look scared?" Vivian shook her head, "No! You look really relaxed!" Darlene affirmed, "Exactly. Trust me, I'm not worried at all." Vivian added, "Do you know if you do this, you will for sure be a hero!!" Confused, Darlene replied, "That's what everyone is saying, but we will see." Turning to her children, Darlene bravely said, "Don't worry about me. Everything is going to be ok." By listening to their mother, the kids stopped crying and left with Vivian.

Darlene sat down for a minute, gathering her thoughts while waiting for the guardsmen to arrive. Thirty minutes later, the guardsmen showed up. They collected Darlene's belongings. Darlene glanced back at her home. One of the four guardsmen consoled her, "Don't worry about your home; we will monitor it and keep it clean until you return." They set off towards the training facility, an hour's drive away. As the guardsmen and Darlene passed by the palace, the Queen, Princess, Lizzes, and the Queen's 35 female staff members were all standing alongside the palace walls, waving at Darlene because they knew what this would mean to all the women in England. Darlene waved back as the carriage disappeared into the distance. As everyone returned to the palace, Lizzes stood there for a few more minutes, reflecting on everything that had happened to get to this point. Turning around, she noticed everyone standing and watching her. Then she walked into the palace. Looking up, she saw the King, Prince, and Earl watching from the window. She continued walking, and both the Queen and Princess locked arms with her as they entered the palace.

CHAPTER 16

CONFUSION OF LANGUAGES

That evening, Lizzes sat in her study with Earl, having a conversation in Portuguese about everything that had happened. Lizzes, cautious not to get too far ahead of herself with her plans, decided to proceed anyway. She expressed to Earl her desire to teach the guardsmen Portuguese and Spanish. Earl immediately objected, "No!" and continued, "You have one guardsman who is willing to learn other things. The other guardsmen, I'm not so sure. The Queen has told you that anything pertaining to the guardsmen must go through her! Why are you being defiant right now?" Lizzes acknowledged, "I know what the Queen said. I'll ask her, but let's ask the guardsman to see what they think about it." Lizzes called in her guardsman on duty and asked him, "I have a question. Would you like to learn Portuguese and Spanish?" The guardsman hesitated and asked, "What is the reason for learning these languages?" Lizzes responded, "The reason is to enhance your skills." She goes on to say, "Wouldn't it be nice to walk around in Spain or Portugal and know the languages? Earl and I will be going home to Portugal for two weeks, where they speak Portuguese." The guardsman declined, stating, "I don't understand the necessity behind creating a different type of guardsmen when we are respected in all of England already." Lizzes shot back, "Exactly, just England, not the world." Lizzes realized she only had one guardsman who was okay with Lizzes idea. Earl suggested pragmatically, "Forget the other three; I just train that one."

Earl continues to say, "Ask the Queen?!!" Lizzes was now stuck. Speaking several languages is a key part of her plan. She decided to accept Earl's advice and train just that one. She would figure out the rest later. She doesn't want to ask the Queen for her approval right now for any of her new ideas until her previous ideas have come forth. She had another plan: she would teach the languages to her co-workers and their children. That night, Lizzes lay awake; it was 2 in the morning. She was anxious about Darlene and how her first day of training had gone. She went to the kitchen to get some water. She heard voices coming from the pantry. She went to see what was going on, and to her surprise, no one was there; the room was empty. A cold chill ran up her arm and back as if she could feel another presence in the room. She saw two figures that looked like white mist—one small and the other tall. Lizzes moved closer as she was afraid and curious at the same time. As she drew near, the two figures vanished into the wall. As Lizzes turned around to walk out of the room, the tall, misty figure appeared right in front of her. Lizzes was startled but wasn't afraid for some reason. Lizzes didn't know what to do as she felt strangely at ease with whatever the mist-like figure was. Compelled, Lizzes reached out to touch the mist, and as she did, it quickly passed through her. As it passed through her, Lizzes realized that whatever the mist was, it was cold but seemed to want her to follow it. The mist moved back into the same wall as before. Lizzes was curious about the wall, so she pushed it just out of curiosity.

The wall opened to reveal a door. The door led to a staircase. There was a switchboard on the side wall, which Lizzes turned on. Lizzes began to walk down the stairs. When she reached the bottom of the stairs, to her surprise, she found two marble stone coffins that looked like they were built within. The only way to take them out was to destroy them. One was small, child-sized, and the other was meant for an adult. Lizzes approached the coffins. She saw pictures on both coffins. On the adult coffin, it was written in a different language. It was a mixture of Spanish, Portuguese, Italian, and Egyptian, all mixed together—and, to Lizzes' astonishment, she could read it! She started reading aloud. The first line reads, "Here lays Princess Doris Buchinham 1756 to 1789—wife of Prince William Buchinham, Daughter of David and Maggot Richards". On the child's coffin, it reads, "Here lays Princess Stacy Buchinham

1780 to 1789. Daughter of Prince William and Doris Buchinham." As Lizzes reads it out loud, the cold room suddenly becomes warm. Lizzes realized the two mist figures had vanished. Realizing she had been gone for about 30 minutes, Lizzes rushed back upstairs. She pushed the trap door and, to her surprise, she found Earl, the guardsmen, and the Royal Family all staring back at her with expressions as astonished as hers.

CHAPTER 17

FORGOTTEN GHOST OF THE PALACE

As Lizzes emerged from the pantry wall, Earl stared in disbelief. He exclaimed, "We have been looking for you for 20 minutes. I woke up, and you were gone and we thought something may have happened to you." The Royal Family was in another phase of mind. Seeing Lizzes emerge into the pantry from the wall left them completely shocked. The Queen remarked, "I'm 52 years old and lived in this palace all of my life and never knew that door was there." She asked Lizzes, "How did you find that door?" Lizzes responded, "Before I tell you that, follow me downstairs." Lizzes pushed open the secret door. Earl, the Royal Family, and two guardsmen followed Lizzes downstairs. Upon reaching the basement, they were all stunned to see two coffins. The Queen and King were in total disarray!!! They couldn't believe their eyes. The King muttered, "Two coffins in a secret basement." He instructed one of the guardsmen, "Retrieve the palace layout from my study's file cabinet." As they examined the coffins, one asked, "Does anyone understand this language?" Lizzes replied confidently, "I understand it, and I can read to you what it says."

Lizzes started reading the inscriptions on the stone coffins. As she read, the Queen smiled at the King, then began to cry. The Prince and Princess asked, "What is all this?" The Queen revealed, "This is my great-great-grandmother and her daughter. They died in this house, but no gravesites were ever found for them. We searched and searched for the gravesites but could never find anything." The King speculated, "There has to be some documentation on why they were buried here." The Queen recalled a story her great-grandmother told about how her mother and sister died after falling down the stairs. She never specified which stairs. Just then, the guardsmen came down the stairs with the layout of the palace. While everyone else was examining the stone coffins, the King brushed off the desk and began to look at the layout of the pantry. He could not find any secret door or room on the layout. He told the Queen, "I think your great-great-grandmother and daughter found the secret door by accident and either fell through the door, went down the stairs, slipped, and died." The Queen decided to make this their gravesite. The Queen then asked Lizzes, "How did you find this door?" Lizzes explained what had happened, leaving the Queen shocked.

The Queen searched around for the two mist figures, but they were nowhere to be seen. Lizzes suggested, "I believe that those figures were your great-great-grandmother and daughter, and now they have finally found peace." The King instructed the guardsmen to take the Queen, Princess and Lizzes back to their rooms. He ordered everyone else to stay behind and start searching for any books, documents, or anything else that would let them know about this secret room. The Prince protested, "Father, it is 3 in the morning. Can't this wait until after breakfast?" The King emphatically replied, "No!!! Start searching!! " At 8 am that morning, Lizzes woke up to find Earl missing. She realized he was still down at the gravesite. She got up and went to the pantry. To her surprise, the pantry was full of about 200 notebocks with writing in a language that no one understood but her. Lizzes opened one of the notebooks and began to read. Lizzes figured out that the books were written by the Queen's great-grandmother. She was amazed at how easily she could read the language. Then, it dawned on her that the Queen would want to read all these notebooks. Lizzes realized she didn't have that kind of time to facilitate that. She now understood that she had to teach this language to the Queen and possibly the entire Royal Family.

Then, the Queen entered the pantry and saw all of the notebooks. She began to open one up, but she couldn't read it. Lizzes' worst thought just came to pass. The Queen handed one to

Lizzes, saying, "Here, read this one for me." Lizzes knew she had to get out of this quickly, or she'd be reading for the Queen all day. Lizzes replied, "Your majesty, I would love to read these books to you, but I think it will be best if I put all these books in order by the dates. And start from the beginning so that you can get a full understanding of what happened and what was going on back in that time." The Queen paused, then said, "Ok, you're right, but how long will that take." Lizzes answered, "Give me three months to work on this cause. The men are still downstairs, finding more material." The Queen glanced at the clock on the wall and said, "They have been down there for about 6 hours now. That's enough for today." The Queen and Lizzes then headed downstairs. The men looked like white ghosts covered in dust. Lizzes and the Queen began to laugh. The Queen announced, "That's enough for today. You can continue tomorrow morning." The Guardsmen, Prince, and Earl all exclaimed at the same time, "Thank God!!" They all made their way back upstairs to wash up for breakfast. The Queen instructed the guardsmen to move everything to Lizzes' study. Lizzes summoned the butler and the Queen's two personal servants to meet her in the study. Lizzes explained that she was going to teach them this language so they could read these books to the Queen, as she didn't have time to do it herself. Lizzes declared, "It will take about three months to teach you how to read this language, and we will start tomorrow morning."

CHAPTER 18

CRITICAL INFORMATION

That evening, around 7 pm, one of Darlene's guardsmen assigned to protect her during training returned to the palace with a report. The guardsman requested Michael, the butler, by saying, "Please go and get Lizzes and the Queen." The butler headed towards the Queen's study and returned with the two ladies. The Queen inquired of the guardsman, "What is it?" The guardsman reported and said, "The trainers and the men are scared to death of Darlene." Lizzes exclaimed, "Scared to death!! Why?" The guardsman explained, "The men think she is the daughter of the devil, and none of the trainers or men want to be around her." The Queen and Lizzes look at each other and burst into laughter so hard that it becomes hysterical. They knew Darlene was putting on an act! Between laughs, the Queen asked the guardsman, "Did she pass her training today?" The guardsman affirmed, "Yes! But she's completely gone crazy! I have seen it with my own eyes." The

Queen wrote a message and handed it to the guardsman. She instructed the guardsman, "Go back and tell the trainers to continue her training as scheduled without any delays."

The guardsman left, and Lizzes and the Queen began to laugh hysterically again. Lizzes turned to the Queen, "Your Majesty. We must go and see this ourselves tomorrow." The Queen responded, "Yes!! I agree." The Queen then asked Lizzes, "Aren't you working tomorrow?" Lizzes replied, "Yes, but the ladies can handle it. I must go and see this for myself." The next morning, the Queen and Lizzes took an hour's trip to the training grounds. No one knew they were coming. When they arrived, the Queen instructed the guardsmen to put them somewhere where no one could see them. As they began to watch the training, they spotted Darlene, and she was out in front of the men during the 5-mile run. She was the first one to cross the finish line. The Queen was stunned; on the other hand, Lizzes was worried!! She was thinking to herself, "How is this woman outworking the men?"

The Queen now seemed to agree with the guardsman that there was something wrong with Darlene. The Queen and Lizzes decided to go down to the grounds and greet the men and Darlene. After greeting the men, they walked over to Darlene. Lizzes looked surprisingly at Darlene and asked, "How is everything going?" Darlene screamingly responded, "I hate it!! I hate everything about this!!" She continued, "But I'm not doing this for you or anyone else. I'm doing this for myself cause all these men said I couldn't do it. So if it looks like I'm angry at everyone, well, I am!! Including you!! So, if you don't mind, I have work to do," she stated bluntly, then walked away.

Lizzes and the Queen were at a loss for words due to Darlene's blatant disrespect. They just walked back to their carriage in shock!! "I don't know who that person is," Lizzes said to the Queen in disbelief. The Queen replied solemnly, "I do. It's the person you and you alone are going to have to deal with when this is over." Lizzes was puzzled, unable to tell if Darlene was acting or not, as the two women made their way back to the palace. The Queen informed the King about Darlene's behavior. The King warned the Queen that Darlene might be transforming into something truly dangerous. "With her anger and rigorous training, she could be a threat to a lot of people," he cautioned. The King instructed, "Once she completes her training, make sure she is closely watched by the guardsmen." That same night, Lizzes told Earl about everything that happened at the training ground with Darlene. Earl alerted Lizzes, "You are creating an individual that you may not be able to control. You should be very careful with Darlene and pray that she doesn't become rebellious. She has a lot of anger towards you, and with that training, she could do a lot of damage!!" Earl added gravely.

◆◆◆

CHAPTER 19

UNIFORMS OF ROYALTY

That morning, Lizzes is excited because she gets to reveal the first of several guardsmen uniforms along with the Royal Family's illustrated drawings for the Princess ball. She must get the Royal Family's approval on her designs so that she can start working immediately on making them. She heads to the workshop and grabs all of the drawings. She distributes one book of drawings to each member of the Royal Family and one to the guardsman who she asks to join at the table. Earl examines Lizzes' book of drawings.

The first drawing features the Princess's dress. It is pearl white with sky-blue outlines. The dress has a V-shaped neckline complemented by a blue and white pearl necklace. The dress also has pearl white lace gloves which stretch up to the forearm. The Princess loved it. The King's and Prince's uniforms were dark Royal Blue adorned with four gold roped straps across the King's right chest and three gold straps across the Prince's right chest. There are gold lace rope straps across the end of each sleeve. Across the left shoulder, there are four gold straps for the King and three gold straps for the Prince. The belt buckle is in the shape of a crown for the King and a smaller crown for the Prince.

The Queen's dress is crafted entirely from gold lace with pearl white outlines, accompanied by a gold necklace and matching white and gold gloves that run all the way to the forearm. The guardsmen's uniform is entirely different. It is light blue with four black outlines at the end of each sleeve. Within the blue outline are pin-like darts that are designed to shoot out one at a time. Inside the coat, each side has two pockets that can hold firearms with bullets. The firearms are four inches in length and three inches wide. The shoes feature two pockets on each side which also have four needle-like darts that only shoot out when the guardsmen make any type of kicking motion. Around the bottom length of the Jacket, twenty 3-inch needles are designed to fly out only when the guardsmen make a fast 360-degree turning motion.

The hat contains four knives in its rim that come flying out when the guardsmen throw it. Additionally, the hat is also a boomerang, and it comes right back to the guardsmen for reloading if necessary. The guardsmen, who were against Lizzes' idea of creating a different guardsman attire, are now excited about the new look. But the King and Queen aren't so much. The King confronts

Lizzes, "What are you trying to create, killers?!!" Lizzes clarifies, "No, my King, only protectors." The Queen probes further, "Protectors of what?" Lizzes explains, "Protectors of the people all over the world." The King and Queen are now understanding Lizzes' intentions. The King questions, "Explain how you're going to protect the people of the world?" Lizzes answers, "By putting well trained guardsmen in every country all over the world that will be able to help people who are in serious or critical crises." The Queen shows a keen interest in Lizzes' plan. She inquires, "When will this plan of yours be ready?" Lizzes estimates, "This plan will take about ten years to implement. The guardsmen will need to go through new training, like learning several languages. Masters in all types of Martial arts and being masters of all weapons." She added, "There is a lot more that will happen, but for now, that's the plan."

The King asks, "Who knows of this plan?" Lizzes assures, "No one, only this table, and that's it!" The King cautions, "We cannot overrun governments, just so you know!!" Lizzes declared, "We want to have to. The government, police officers, judges, and lawyers will be mostly the world guardsmen, and once all country governments realize our purpose and how powerful the guardsmen are, they will not interfere with our purpose of helping people in crises when their country's leader lets them down." The Queen warns, "Prepare for a political and physical fight because once this plan is implemented, governments will fight against you." Lizzes confidently asserts, "We will be ready when that day comes." The Queen accepts, "You have my approval." The King interjects, "Hold on!! How will you fund this plan?" Lizzes replies, "I have an idea."

CHAPTER 20

FOUNDATION OF FUNDS

That evening, Lizzes finds Earl in their study and tells him that she needs to talk. She queries Earl, "What do you think of the idea of turning our home into a non-profit organization?" Earl asks, "What do you mean?" Lizzes explains, "I have an idea of how to fund the plan." Earl remarked, "By turning our home into a non-profit organization?" Lizzes elaborates, "Yes! We can cook food and buy supplies for the homeless and people in need of help, and we can ask other businesses like coffee shops and working-class people to donate to our cause, and we can do it out of our homes." Earl objects, "No!" Lizzes protests, "No! Why?" Earl explains, "Because that's our home, and we're going to need a place to go if you continue to test the King and Queen's authority and patience." Lizzes reassures, "The Royal Family loves us. They would never kick us out." Earl replies, "Yeah, keep thinking that." He suggests, "How about going into town and renting out office space?" Lizzes considers, "I'll look into it, but I would rather use our home to start the process."

Earl firmly repeats, "No!" Lizzes exclaims, "Fine," and stomps out. Earl continues to read his book. Lizzes walks back in, snatches her notepad, and Earl inquires, "By the way, what are you going to name this non-profit?" Lizzes announces, "Blessed the People Foundation!!" Earl pauses and then shoots back, "I like that. Let me know when you want to go into town and look for office space." Lizzes gives Earl an angry look and storms out, frustrated because she really wants to use their home, although she knows Earl isn't going to go for it. Fifteen minutes later, the butler enters and informs Earl, "Lizzes will be ready to go into town to look at office space in 30 minutes." Earl responds, "Ok, and thank you."

Earl, Lizzes, and the guardsmen enter the town and immediately find the perfect place for the Non-profit. It has a kitchen and a small lunchroom that can accommodate 25 to 50 people. It also has three rooms for other necessities. Lizzes instructed one of the guardsmen to remove the for-rent sign and find out who owns the building. Lizzes and Earl decide to take a joy ride around town. They approach a part of town that they have not been to. The guardsman tries to make a detour, but Lizzes tells him to keep going. The guardsman cautions, "That's not a good idea. This is the segregated part of town. This is where all the black people live." Lizzes gives the guardsman an angry glare. Lizzes sharply asks, "Did you forget that we are black?" The guardsman replies, "No, I did not, but you are Royalty now, and you don't look black." Lizzes warns the guardsman, "You and I will have a conversation later." The guardsman glances at Earl. Earl shakes his head at the guardsman, telling him to leave it alone without even speaking. They enter the segregated part of town and are surprised to find many black-owned businesses.

Lizzes exclaims, "Stop!!" upon seeing a black man leaving a building that has a rent sign on it. She stops and asks the gentleman, "Who is the owner of the building?" The gentleman replies, "The country of England owns this building and a lot more." Lizzes asks, "Who is the manager of this building?" The gentleman answers, "I am." Lizzes requests, "May we look at the space for rent." The gentleman hesitates, "Excuse me, but may I ask who you are? You don't look like you belong in this part of town." Lizzes smiles and assures, "Oh, we belong…" Lizzes tells the gentleman who they are, and upon hearing this, the gentleman immediately starts to treat them like a member of the Royal Family. Lizzes tells the gentleman, "That's not necessary."

Lizzes asks the gentleman again if they could see the rental space. The gentleman agrees and says, "Yes," then unlocks the door and lets them in. The rental space has everything Lizzes needs. She informs the gentleman that she will take it and requests to start the paperwork. The guardsmen express concern, "This isn't a good idea." Lizzes ignores the guardsmen and inquires of the gentleman, "Do you know of any women who would like a job?" The gentleman responds affirmatively, "Yes, how many?" Lizzes specifies, "3 to start." She continues, "Tell them to meet me here at 10 am tomorrow morning." The gentleman confirms, "I will make sure they are here." He hands the paperwork to Lizzes. Earl and Lizzes read over the paperwork before signing it. Lizzes queries the gentleman, "Could you have a sign made to look like this!?" Then, Lizzes sketches a sign with the words 'Blessed the People Foundation' encircling the world globe on it. The gentleman says, "Yes, I know someone." Lizzes requests the gentleman, "Please have the sign here in 3 days. For now, I will tape the paper to the windows with the business name on it." Lizzes thanks the gentleman, saying, "Thank you, and I'll see you tomorrow." As Earl and Lizzes begin to walk out of the building with the gentleman, the two guardsmen standing outside make eye contact with the two inside. All four immediately go into protect mode and are on high alert. Puzzled, Lizzes and Earl are wondering what's going on.

CHAPTER 21

CRUELTY OF A SEGREGATED PEOPLE

Earl and Lizzes are waiting inside the building, and the two guardsmen with them won't let them out. They look out the window and a crowd has gathered in front of the building. Lizzes and Earl can see the crowd is having a conversation with the two guardsmen outside. The gentleman glances outside and assures Lizzes and Earl, "The crowd is just curious. They don't get Royal Family members to come visit in this part of town." The gentleman added, "Let me go outside and talk to them." The gentleman goes outside, and another gentleman from the crowd inquires, "What are members of the Royal Family doing in this part of town? We haven't seen a Member of the Royal Family in Decades in this part of town."

The gentleman explains, “They’re here to open up a business in this building.” The crowd grows agitated, and everyone is screaming and yelling, “We don’t want you here. You don’t belong here.” Lizzes being Lizzes, decided she’d heard enough. She commands the guardsmen who blocked her path, “Move.” The guardsmen caution, “It’s not safe out there.” Lizzes firmly orders, “Step aside! Now!” The guardsmen move slightly. Once Lizzes and Earl step outside, the crowd gets even more agitated. Addressing the crowd, Lizzes pleads, “Can you please calm down for a moment, please?” As the crowd calms down, Lizzes asks the gentleman in the crowd who is making the most noise, “Please step forward.” She inquires, “Good evening, Sir. My name is Lizzes, and this is my husband, Earl. May I ask your name?” The gentleman replies, “My name is Allen.”

“Nice to meet you, Allen.” She continues, “What is the issue with us not being wanted in this part of town?” Allen explains, “First, we black people are welcome to go and work for the white bosses, but we’re not welcome to socialize in the white part of town. As soon as our work is done, we have to leave and come to be with our people here.” Allen continues to say, “No one from the Royal Family has been here in years. So now you show up with your guardsmen wanting to start a business in the segregated black part of town.” He adds, “You don’t belong here.”

“You’re not black!!” The crowd starts screaming again.

Lizzes glances at Earl, who has this "Ah hell" look on his face because he knows what's about to happen. Lizzes addresses Allen, "Well, just so you know, we are part of the Royal Family, so we can go anywhere in this country as we please whether you like it or not. So I'm going to ask you nicely to calm down so we can have a peaceful conversation."

The guardsmen take a step forward, prompting the crowd to step back. Lizzes asks Allen, "Can we have a peaceful conversation?" Allen looks at the guardsmen and agrees, "Yes." Then, the guardsmen step back. "Just so you know," She continues, "Both of our fathers are black, and our mothers are Portuguese. So yeah, we are black!!" The crowd falls silent and has this unbelievable look on their faces. Allen, stunned, asks Lizzes and Earl, "You're black?" Lizzes confirms, "Yes." Allen, puzzled, remarks, "You don't look black, and you are a member of the Royal Family?" Lizzes replies, "Yes!" She opens her purse and pulls out her and Earl's birth certificates and shows them to Allen. He hands the birth certificates back to Lizzes and begins to immediately praise aloud, "God, Thank you!" Turning to the people, he proclaims, "God hasn't forgotten us. This is a sign from God!!" Lizzes and Earl observe as the crowd's anger now turns to tears.

Lizzes turns at the building manager, apologizing, "I'm sorry for not asking earlier, but what is your name?" The building manager introduces himself, "My name is Donald West. The people call me Don." Lizzes inquires Don, "What is going on?" Don explains to Lizzes, "We have been asking and praying to God for a sign of hope! And you are a sign of hope that there is a future for us black people." Don shakes hands with Earl and Lizzes, and so does the crowd. Fifteen minutes pass by, and the guardsmen step in and tell Earl and Lizzes, "It's time to go." They leave with the crowd walking behind, cheering and waving. Earl comments, "I hope it's not like this tomorrow." Lizzes responds, "We will see." Later that night at the palace in their study, Earl tells Lizzes, "I think you need to slow down. You have a lot going on. We do have a child, you know." At that moment, Lizzes writes down all that she has to do.

Recap:

- 1. Royal clothing for the Princess ball.
- 2. Guardsmen's new uniforms.
- 3. Teaching her coworkers and their children Portuguese and Spanish.
- 4. Darlene and her training.
- 5. Teaching the butler and the Queen's two personal servants the languages of the Queen's great great-grandmother. So they can read to the Queen the 200-plus notebooks found in the pantry basement.
- 6. Giving her writings to the butler to hide in their home.
- 7. Opening her non-profit in the segregated part of town.

Earl requests Lizzes, “Let me see your list.” Earl reads over the list, and he inquires, “What’s number 6 all about?” Lizzes suddenly realized that she had just been caught keeping a secret from Earl!!!

CHAPTER 22

SECRETS, LIES, AND AFFAIRS

Lizzes realizes she has just been caught keeping a secret from Earl. So, Lizzes confesses to Earl about her secret writings. She tells him, “These writings consist of everything that happens in the palace and outside of the palace.” She also tells him about the new language she is writing. Earl interjects, “I don’t care about that! What I care about is you keeping a secret from me!! Me of all people!”

Earl is highly upset! He storms out of the study and heads to the guest room. Lizzes knows she has made a huge mistake. She picks up the baby and also makes her way towards the guest room. To her surprise, Earl has locked the door. She apologizes, “I’m sorry, and it won’t happen again.” Earl opens up the door. He’s still visibly upset and says sternly, “I accept your apology, but the baby and I will be sleeping in the guest room tonight, and you can sleep alone.” Earl takes the baby from Lizzes, says goodnight, and slams the door in Lizzes' face. She returns to the bedroom with tears streaming down her face. She cried all night until she finally fell asleep. The next morning, everyone is at breakfast except Lizzes. Five minutes later, Lizzes shows up. Her eyes are puffy and red from crying all night, and everyone notices it. The Queen inquires, "Lizzes are you ok? Your eyes are red and puffy, like you've been crying all night." Lizzes, stammers, "I…I don't know. Is everything ok, Earl?"

Earl looks at Lizzes and reassures, "Yes, everything is ok." After breakfast, Earl gets ups and says, "Excuse me, I have to get to work." Lizzes quickly stands and runs after him. The King turns to the Queen, asking, "What do you think Lizzes did this time?" The Queen smiles and responds, "I don't know, but I know whatever she did, Earl is very upset about it." Catching up to Earl, Lizzes pleads, "Please forgive me. I promise I will never keep anything away from you again." Earl states, "I already accepted your apology, but know this, if you ever keep anything from me again, our daughter and I will leave you here in this palace and stay in our home." At that moment, Lizzes becomes actually frightened. Earl has never ever said that he would leave. Earl walks off. Lizzes sadly takes the baby to the nursery. Then, she goes to the workshop and informs her three co-workers that she will not be working today.

She dresses and heads to the kitchen where Earl is. She asks Earl, "Are you coming with me to meet the three ladies in the segregated part of town?"

"No," Earl says bluntly. "You can handle it." She turns away, and Earl can see she's visibly hurt! She mutters, "Ok," and departs. As Lizzes and the guardsmen exit the kitchen, one of the lady servants walks past Earl, and they smile at each other. The guardsmen see both of them and stop, giving Earl a look of disbelief. One of the guardsmen signals the other guardsmen to go, and he will catch up. He walks up to Earl. The entire kitchen staff stops what they're doing. They are aware that the guardsmen don't do this, so they know it's serious. He gets nose to nose with Earl, who now is frightened to death because he hasn't seen this aggression from any of the guardsmen. He tells Earl, "I saw the interaction between you and the young lady." The guardsman sternly warns, "Whatever that was, it ends now!!" The guardsman demands, "Are we clear??" Earl, who is scared to death, says, "Yes!!!" The guardsman then instructs Earl, "Go change and accompany your wife into town today. We will be waiting for you outside."

Earl walks fast out of the kitchen. The guardsman looks at the kitchen staff, who is looking at him. They all turn their heads and resume their work. The guardsman goes outside and tells the other guardsmen about what happened, and they become upset, also. Lizzes notices the interaction between the guardsmen and ask,

"What happened?" The guardsman explains, "There was a disagreement in the kitchen, but it's taken care of now." Earl comes walking out and joins Lizzes in the carriage while the guardsmen are staring at him intently. Seeing this, Lizzes tells Earl, "I don't know what happened, and I don't want to know." Lizzes inquires, "Is everything ok now?" Earl confirms, "Yes!" And gives Lizzes a kiss! The guardsmen then turn away and head into town.

Earl is now holding Lizzes' hand tightly, and Lizzes realizes that it is a 'scared-to-death grip and a love hand hold' at the same time. She knows something happened between Earl and the guardsmen, but she chooses to leave it alone because whatever it was, the guardsmen took care of it. They enter into town and reach the building that they want to rent. The guardsmen had found out who owned the building and set up a meeting for Earl and Lizzes. As Lizzes and Earl are surveying the building, the owner of the building asks them about their race and where they are from. Lizzes declares, "We are from Portuguese, and of African descent."

After hearing that they are of African descent, the gentleman refuses to rent the building to Lizzes and Earl. The guardsmen begin to step in and discipline the gentleman, but Lizzes stops him. She tells the gentleman, "Thank you for your time," and then signals everyone to go. Earl is furious and suggests to Lizzes, "We should tell the Queen what happened." Lizzes insisted, "No! We can't have the Queen fighting our battles for us. We already have a building rented in the segregated part of town. We will get that one started and work on getting another building to rent later." Thirty minutes later, they reach the segregated part of town, and about 200 people are waiting for them.

The word has gotten out that members of the Royal Family are black. They enter into the building. The three ladies are there to meet Lizzes and Earl. They all bow to Lizzes, and she immediately stops them. Lizzes requests, "Please do not bow to me." The ladies protest, "But you are royalty." Lizzes explains, "Yes, but we are still black, and when people find out we're black, they treat us accordingly, so please don't bow." The ladies understood and said, "Ok, we are sorry." Lizzes tells the ladies about her plan for the building and that supplies will start to arrive in a couple of days. She hands the ladies two weeks' advance salary. The ladies look at each other with smiles on their faces and express their gratitude, saying, "Thank you!!!" Lizzes apologizes, "I'm so sorry I am bad with names. What are your ladies' names?" The ladies introduce themselves one by one, and their names are Jacqueline, Eleanor, and Bridgett. Lizzes acknowledges their names and introduces herself, "I'm Lizzes, and this is my husband, Earl. Nice to meet you." The ladies respond likewise.

Lizzes asks the ladies, "Do you know anyone who would like to do security 24 hours?" The ladies respond, "Yes." Lizzes specifies, "Ok, I need four gentlemen in the morning, four in the evening, and four at night." She instructs the ladies, "Have the gentleman meet me here tomorrow morning." Lizzes fears that there will be trouble when racist people find out about her non-profit organization in the segregated part of town. Lizzes and Earl leaves and heads back to the palace. As they ride through town, they notice people staring at them. The word is out that they are really black. In that moment, Lizzes realizes what she has to do.

CHAPTER 23

THE COLOR GUARD

That night, Lizzes informs Earl, "I'm going to train all races as guardsmen, starting with the black race." Earl advises, "You may want to ask the Queen before you do that." Lizzes ignores his statement and counters, "Remember on the boat ride here to England; those three Chinese men were practicing martial arts?" Earl recalls, "Yes, the ones who got off in Bordeaux?" Lizzes continues, "Yes, remember they had a lot of equipment and supplies with them. I think they were setting up some type of martial arts school." Earl agrees, "Yes, probably. They had crowds of people on that boat, giving them money when they were practicing." Lizzes declares, "Yes, I'm going to send ten guardsmen to Bordeaux to find them tomorrow." Earl points out, "That's a week there and a week back." Lizzes confirms, "Yes, I know, but I need to find them."

That morning, Lizzes gets up early and sends ten guardsmen to Bordeaux to find the Chinese men. She also hands her writings to the butler to take to her home. She's very excited about her non-profit organization. This non-profit organization will provide the financing to pay for her future plans. As she heads back to bed, she runs into the Princess. The Princess requests a moment with Lizzes, asking, "May I speak with you?" Lizzes replies, "Of course." The Princess reveals, "I know you sent ten guardsmen to Bordeaux to find three Chinese men. Why come you didn't ask the Queen's permission to send the guardsmen?" Lizzes explains, "I didn't think it was serious enough to involve the Queen." The Princess asserted, "But it is serious!! If the Queen finds out you sent those guardsmen on a mission without her permission, she will be very upset with you."

"I will approve this mission, but from now on, you will clue me in when it comes to the guardsmen just so you don't get in any trouble with the Queen." The Princess added. Lizzes agrees, adding, "But just remember, the guardsmen will let the Royal Family know anything and everything when they are involved." They conclude their conversation, and Lizzes heads back to bed, where Earl overhears the conversation and remarks, "You will always do things the hard way, and that's going to get you in trouble." At that moment Lizzes knows she must have to create her version of guardsmen where she will be in charge and won't have to answer to anyone.

That morning, after breakfast Lizzes and Earl pass the coffee shop on their way to the nonprofit office. Just as Lizzes expects, people are staring out the window and in the streets at them. Lizzes is visibly upset. She tells the guardsmen to turn around and take them to the coffee shop. Lizzes decides to show her power. As they enter the coffee shop, they sit down at a table. The coffee shop manager, who knows Lizzes and Earl very well, apologizes, "I'm sorry, Lizzes, but can you and Earl sit in the black part of the restaurant in the back? This is the white section of the restaurant." Lizzes firmly says, "No!" She continues to tell the store manager, "For two years, you thought I was white, and there was no problem with me sitting here. Now that you found out I'm black, you treat me disrespectfully even though you know I'm a member of the Royal Family." The manager explains, "I know, but the people are getting upset."

So, Lizzes decides to show the manager her Royal power. She instructs the guardsmen to kick everyone out of the restaurant except her, Earl, and the black people in the back. She states, "If they don't want to sit with us black people, they can go somewhere else and have coffee." The manager is in disbelief, and Lizzes decides to scold the manager, "You take our money, which is the same money that they, the white people, have, but you treat us differently because of the color of our skin." She declares, "Fine, every day from now on; they can wait until we leave to come in. As a matter of fact, I'm reserving this section of the restaurant from 6 am to 8 am every morning for myself and the black people. They can come in after we leave." She instructs the guardsmen to go and tell the white people outside of the changes while Lizzes and Earl have their coffee.

The manager protests to Lizzes and Earl, "You can't do this!!" Lizzes retorts, "Oh really, watch me," she warns the manager. "If we show up tomorrow and people are sitting in our section between 6 am and 8 am, I will have them kicked out again." She goes on to say, "If you decide to close between those hours, I will have this coffee shop closed down permanently, and you will not be able to open a coffee shop anywhere in this country." Just then, the Princess and Prince show up at the coffee shop, and the crowd begins screaming, complaining, and yelling at them about what just happened. The Prince asks Lizzes and Earl's guardsmen about what happened.

The guardsmen explain the situation. Upon hearing, the Princess starts smiling and goes into the coffee shop, sits with Lizzes, and asks the manager for coffee. The Prince informs the crowd that the coffee shop will reopen to them at 8 am and wishes them a good day. The crowd is in disbelief but now understands Lizzes' power. Lizzes directs the manager to get the black people from the back and have them sit in her section until 8 am. The black people smile appreciatively. Lizzes goes to the black people and apologizes, "I'm sorry that you are being treated with no respect, and I'm sorry for just now doing something about it. I promise you things will change." Lizzes continues, "I know you work for the white bosses in town, cleaning their homes and cooking for them. Whatever your work is for the white bosses, if you get any backlash from them, let me know."

Lizzes and Earl leave the coffee shop at 8 am. The Princess and Prince head back to the palace. Once the doors open, the people outside enter the coffee shop, visibly angry. They start screaming at the manager and at his service staff. Frustrated, the manager exclaims, "What do you want me to do? They are the Royal Family. Leave it alone and drink your coffee." Lizzes and Earl arrive at the nonprofit office. The three ladies have six men waiting for Lizzes to meet. Lizzes instructs the guardsmen to collect identification from all the men. Then, the guardsmen escort the six men to the back of the room.

One of the ladies asks, "What are they going to do with them?" Lizzes explains, "Just making sure they understand the consequences and actions of the job." Five minutes later, the six men come back into the front of the building, scared to death!! Lizzes inquires of the men, "Do you understand the consequences?" The men replied, "Yes!" Lizzes questioned, "Do you still want the job?" They respond, "Yes!!" Lizzes affirms, "Good." The guardsmen give the men guns with their protection sealed on them, along with the sealed letter that they each signed in the back room.

The guardsmen inform the six men, "You are now protected by the guardsmen and can go anywhere in the country as you please. If anyone tries to harm you or your family, show them this letter with the guardsmen sealed and show them the gun with our seal. If they continue to try and do harm, start a fire and take this blue dye; throw it in the fire. The fire will turn blue, and that will signal nearby guardsmen." The guardsmen then request the men to step outside. They go outside and see six of the finest horses with the guardsmen seals on the horses. They told the six men to only travel on roads that are marked with horse travel in the back and side roads in the city. The six men are extremely nervous. They have no idea how people are going to react to them, but they know backlash from people will come.

CHAPTER 24

TESTED BUT RESPECTED

Earl and Lizzes return to the palace. The Queen invites Lizzes and the Princess to meet in her study.

She announces, “We have a new way of transportation. We will be riding in the new automobile in and around town. The roads are going to be smoothed out for the travel of the automobile. Each of you will have your own.” The Princess and Lizzes get extremely excited about the way of traveling. They are also relieved because they thought that the Queen wanted to know what happened at the coffee shop. As the Princess and Lizzes walk out of the Queen’s study, Lizzes asks the Princess, “Do you think she knows about the coffee shop?” The Princess replies, “Yes.” Lizzes is curious about why the Queen didn’t address the incident at the coffee shop. She lets it go and heads to the work area to check on her coworkers. She is surprised to find the ladies working extremely hard to get all the clothing designs together. Lizzes apologizes to the ladies for not helping.

She explains, “I have a lot of projects going on, and I just can’t be in one place all day.” She reviews the designs and loves them all. The ladies announce to Lizzes, “We have a surprise for you.” The ladies unveil a new design for Darlene. It’s a superb outfit, similar to the men’s but more feminine. Lizzes loves it. She informed the ladies, “Darlene’s training ends in seven weeks. It’s January 30, 1901, and she may not make it.” The ladies assure her, “She will make it, and when she does, we want her outfits to be ready.” Lizzes grants the ladies full control over the work area. Lizzes then goes to her study to meet Earl for lunch. Upon entering, she finds the King and Queen already there to have lunch with them.

The King inquires Lizzes, “Why did you open your nonprofit in the segregated area of town and not the in-town area?” Lizzes explains, “I wanted to open one in both areas, but the manager of the building in town found out that we were black and decided not to rent the building to us.” Infuriated, the King and Queen ordered the guardsmen on duty to find the manager and the owner of the building. The King wants to speak with them personally. Lizzes pleads, “Please, King, I appreciate you wanting to help, but we can’t run to you and the Queen every time we have a problem. We have to handle this one on our own.”

The Queen's fury is palpable. Lizzes soothes, "My Queen, I can see that you are upset, but we are black, and the people know it now, and we will be treated accordingly to a certain extent whether we are Royalty or not. The people won't give us our respect anymore. We will have to make them respect us now." The Queen inquires, "Is that what happened this morning at the coffee shop?" Lizzes smiles and says, "Yes." The Queen responds, "I have something for you and Earl." The King calls for the Princess and Prince to come in. The Princess hands an envelope to the Queen. She opens it. She begins reading the letter aloud. The letter confirms on this day, January 30, 1901, that Lizzes and Earl are adopted by the Queen and King. They are now Duke and Duchess and the official members of the Royal Family. Earl and Lizzes are in complete shock! Even though they have the respect of a family member, it was never official. Now it is.

The Princess and Lizzes are crying like little babies. The letter further states their baby will be given the title of Princess Lizzie from now on and recognized as a granddaughter of the King and Queen. At that moment, Earl tries to hold it in, but he can't, and he begins to cry like a baby himself. There will be a ceremony. The ceremony is set for February 27th, 1901, at the palace. The Queen commands the guardsmen to make a notification of this letter worldwide. The King and Queen see how overwhelmed Lizzes and Earl are; they allow them to sign the letter and leave it to themselves.

Shortly thereafter, the guardsmen come in and inform Lizzes and Earl that their presence is requested outside in the palace roadway in 30 minutes. They acknowledge the guardsmen with an "Okay, and thank you." They gather their senses, get the baby, who is now Princess Lizzie, and head outside.

They see the new automobiles that have just been delivered to them from the England automobile manufacturer. Drivers are present there to take the Royal Family on a drive around the city. The guardsmen will be on horses riding aside them. They all enter their automobiles and begin their ride around town. The Princess and Prince are leading, and the King and Queen are in the middle. Lizzes and Earl trailing with guardsmen on the sides, front, and back of the Royal Family. As they enter town the crowd begins to wave and cheer them. The Royal Family waves back, except Earl and Lizzes. They don't know what to do, knowing the racism in the city. The lead guardsmen see their confusion and instruct them to wave back. Following his instruction, they wave. Although they receive respect from the people, Lizzes and Earl are curious if that same respect will be given when they are not with the King and Queen.

As they are riding alone, the lead guardsmen tell Lizzes to look up. Lizzes looks up, and to her surprise, they are heading in the direction of the segregated area. As they enter the segregated area, the black people on the streets stop and begin to watch. Recognizing Lizzes and Earl, they start waving and cheering. They stop at the nonprofit office. The Royal Family gets out of their automobiles and approaches the security guards, who are well-dressed and standing at the entrance of the nonprofit. They bow to the Royal Family. The guardsmen ask for their papers with the guardsmen's seal on them. The guards present the papers to the Queen and King. They look over the papers and return them back to the security guards. The guardsmen then ask them to show their weapons with the guardsmen's seal on it. The guards display their weapons.

The King and Queen look over the weapons. They give the weapons back and shake hands with the security guards, who bow back to the Royal Family. The guards step aside. The Royal Family enters the nonprofit office. The Queen looks back at Lizzes with a smile of approval. The security guards look at Lizzes with a smile on their faces as she walks by. Lizzes smiles back in approval. They enter the nonprofit; the Royal Family is amazed by the decorations and office design. They approach the young ladies who are also well dressed and professional looking. The ladies bow to the Royal Family. They are surprised that the Royal Family is here. The Queen asks the ladies, "What are you working on?" One of the ladies, Bridget, says, "I'm working on menus for feeding the people in need." Jacqueline, the other lady, mentions, "I'm working on flyers to hand out to businesses that would like to donate to the nonprofit." Eleanor adds, "I'm working on payroll and cost to give to Lizzes and Earl at the end of each week." The Queen smiles at Lizzes and remarks, “Very interesting.” She continues, “Have a nice day, ladies. It was a pleasure to meet you.”

As they exit the nonprofit, Lizzes gives the ladies a big smile and a silent nod of thanks. While entering their automobiles, Lizzes inquires of the Princess, “Does she know everything that’s going on?” The Princess responds sarcastically, “Yes, she does!!!” They enter their automobiles, and one of the guardsmen comes back to Lizzes and Earl and asks, “The Queen wants to know how long will it be before you have a black man and black woman training as guardsmen?” Lizzes is in complete shock, feeling like the Queen is in her head. Earl laughs while Lizzes replies uncertainly, “I don’t know yet, not long, maybe a month.” The guardsmen leave to relay the message to the Queen. Earl remarks, “Even though it’s been only a couple of months living in the palace, the Queen knows you very well!” He continues to laugh. They proceed with their trip around the city. As they are driving through the segregated part of the city, they see how clean this part of town is. They see a sign that says ‘Greater Landing.’ The Queen questions the King, “This area is part of London. Why are they calling it Greater Landing?” The King replies, “That is a good question for Lizzes to find out.” They keep driving and can’t help but notice how pretty everything is. There is no horse waste on the roads or any smell of horses anywhere. As they make their way back to the palace, they can tell the difference between the two areas. Meanwhile, Lizzes sees how clean Greater Landing is and comes up with another idea.

◆◆◆

CHAPTER 25

THE FIRST CITY

That evening, Earl and Lizzes are in their study, and Princess Lizzie is playing on the floor. Lizzes expresses to Earl, "I don't want my daughter growing up in racism." Earl responds, "At some point in time in the future, she will experience it." Lizzes replies, "I know, but I still don't want her growing up in that atmosphere." Earl questioned, "I don't know how you can prevent that?" Lizzes suggests, "Wouldn't it be nice to have a place where racism is not allowed?" Earl asks, "How can you do that?" Lizzes advises, "What if we build up Greater Landing to the point where it's the best town in the country? Everyone will want to come there to shop and eat. It will be mostly like a tourist attraction. But racism is not allowed, and the guardsmen will be the police." Earl notes, "Outlawing racism in a particular area will have to be a law passed by the Parliament." Lizzes states, "I know, the Queen is part of the Parliament."

Earl cautions, "That doesn't mean she will side with you. You will have to show proof of the law that you want passed." Lizzes inquires, "What do you mean proof?" Earl asserts, "You are going to have to make it impossible for the parliament to say no!" Lizzes declares, "Well, let's make it impossible for them to say no." Earl accepts, "Ok, what's the first step?" Lizzes explains, "We have taken the first step. We open a business in Greater Landing. The next step is to secure the area. We need to hire at least 200 security guards for now. There are racist people in town, and once they find out what's going on in Greater Landing, they will try and stop it." That night, she had a dream. Lizzes dreams she is in America with Princess Lizzie. They are in a city that is 10 miles long in each direction.

The city is surrounded by a 20-foot wall that has guardsmen posted along the wall. Inside the city, there are smaller replicas of other major cities around the world. The city's population is about 1.5 million, and racism is not allowed. It was a holy place and all races lived there with the religion of their choice. There is an airport that had the guardsmen's seal on it. The laws of the land are based on the 'Ten Commandments.' If you broke any of these laws and after being convicted three times in one year, you would be exiled out of the city. After one year, your conviction will be taken off your record. Each law broken carries a fine from 5000 to 500,000 dollars, depending on the severity. There are no judges, police, or government parties in the city, just the guardsmen. All the businesses inside the city are owned by Lizzes' family members. Wages inside the city are 50 to 65 dollars an hour. There are no taxes. There is free health care for everyone inside the city. The money had Lizzes and Earl's faces on it and some other family member's face that she couldn't see.

The bills are colored in purple, white, and blue, and each is valued at 100 times more than any other currency in the world. One Penny has the value of five American dollars. People who live in the city have a passport to every country in the world. When visiting other cities in America or the world, they must respect the laws of the cities they are visiting. If they break any laws, they will be deported back to their country, where these offenses will stay on their record. They would also pay a fine to the city or country where the law or laws are broken before they could enter that country or city again. The people traveling outside the city had 2 to 4 city guardsmen representatives with them at all times who would handle all interactions when confronted with the other city government officials. If any city member is framed by any outside government officials in any city or country, then the person or persons who did the wrong against a city member would be turned over to the guardsmen.

After being identified by other city officials or people, the city member or members are usually left alone. There are no coins as money—only paper. There are 20 banks with the name World City Bank. All city member's automobiles have license plates that read WORLDM on them. Their passports are their driving licenses. Every city member has a license to carry in any country.

And then, Lizzes wakes up. She hurries up and writes down everything she just dreamed. Then she wakes Earl up and reads to him what she dreamed. Lizzes tells Earl, "Tomorrow, we need to go to the city and find out who owns all those empty abandoned buildings in Greater Landing. If the Country of England owns them all, we need to try and buy them." Earl responds, "There are 10 to 15 abandoned buildings in that area. That's a lot of money and buildings." Lizzes assures, "We don't have to buy them right now. We just need to know who owns them and if they are willing to sell them." Earl shot back Lizzes, "Enough, go back to sleep; it's 3 am. We can talk about this tomorrow."

That morning the security guards decide to test their newfound authority. They decide to ride their horses into the city and go to the coffee shop. At 6 am, they are surprised to find the coffee shop filled with black people. As they got off their horses, five white gentlemen approached them with their hands on their guns. They ask the black security guards, "Where did you steal those horses and those clothes from? Cause they are not yours." They order the security guards to hand over the horses and don't move. They tell one of the men to go and get the police. Two of the white men approach the security guards to seize the horses and hold them until the police arrive. The security guards warn them to back off. "We are protected by the guardsmen," they declared. The white men begin to laugh and say, "No, you're not. Stop lying and hand over those horses." The security guards refuse, saying firmly, "No! Back off." The security guards display their papers with the guardsmen's seal and their guns, also marked with the guardsmen's seal. The white guys step back with guns drawn, and all the while, the black people in the coffee shop watch intently. They shout at the security guards, "You thieves!!" Just then, shots are fired!!! The people in the coffee shop hit the floor. Both security guards are shot multiple times but are still alive.

The police arrive to find the two security guards on the ground, bleeding. The white men tell the police they have stolen guns with the guardsmen seals on them and false papers signed by the guardsmen. The police see the guns and the papers with seals and immediately know the security guards didn't steal them. The police chief orders two of his officers to arrest the five white men and the other two police officers to help get the security guards to the doctors. The Chief confronts the white men, "You are in serious trouble. Did you even read the papers?" One gentleman retorts, "No! We didn't need to, cause they were stolen." The police counter, "They were not stolen. They are signed by the security guards and the guardsmen." The officer warns the men, "You better pray that they don't die!" Two officers rush the wounded security guards to the doctor's office. The doctor refuses to help, saying, "We don't operate on black people, and they have their own doctors for that. Take them to their doctors." The police officer argues, "They will die before we get them to that part of the town. You need to operate now!!"

The doctor still refuses! The police officer shows the doctors the papers with the guardsmen's seal on them. They explain, "These two men are protected by the guardsmen. If they die and the guardsmen find out you wouldn't operate to save them, you will be arrested by the guardsmen." Reluctantly, the doctor agrees to operate and instructs his nurses to prepare themselves. Meanwhile, the five white men now realize they have made a very bad mistake. They knock the police officers to the ground and take off running. The chief police officer tells his men not to go after them. "The guardsmen will be on their tail now," he assures.

CHAPTER 26

GUARDSMEN OF FURY

Meanwhile, the chief police officer arrives at the palace and informs the guardsmen on duty about what just happened. The guardsmen ask for descriptions of the five gentlemen. The police officer asks, "What would you like us to do?" The guardsman responds, "Nothing, we will take it from here."

At the time, Lizzes, Earl, the Princess, and the Prince head toward the guardsmen at the door on their way to the coffee shop. They see him talking to the police officer. The guardsmen thank the police officer and close the door. He turns around, and Lizzes can see something is wrong written all over his face. She inquires of the guardsmen, "What's wrong?" The guardsmen explain, "Your two security guards were shot at the coffee shop and are at the doctor's in town being operated on as we speak." The Royal Family, enraged, instructs the guardsmen to take them to the doctor's office. The family reaches the doctor's office, and they rush in. The nurse on duty is shocked to see the Royal Family there worried about two black men. Lizzes asks, “How are the men doing?” The nurse replies, “I don’t know; they are both being operated on at the same time in different rooms.” She goes on to say, “You are welcome to wait in the waiting room.” Lizzes replies, “Thank you.” As they are waiting in the room, the doctor’s staff is all confused and talking about why the Royal Family would be so concerned about these men. Two nurses enter the doctor’s office and inform both the doctors and nurses who are performing the surgery that the Royal Family is in the waiting room. They all pause and realize this is more serious than they all thought. Two hours later, both doctors come out to greet the Royal Family. They informed the family that both men had several gunshot wounds but are in stable condition right now. “We just have to wait and let their bodies do the rest,” they conclude.

Lizzes gets up and instructs the doctors to take really good care of those two men. “I’m putting guardsmen on duty around the clock to make sure they are taken care of,” she adds. The doctors assure, “We will make sure they are taken care of.” As they’re leaving the doctor’s office, the Princess asks the guardsmen, “What happened?” The guardsmen explain the incident. She commands, “Take 20 guardsmen and hunt those men down, and when you find them, bring them to me by all means necessary.” The Royal Family heads to the coffee shop while the lead guardsmen return to the palace to prepare the guardsmen. Upon arriving at the coffee shop, they find it filled with white customers. The family walks in, and everyone gets quiet. Lizzes declares, "I know you all seen or heard what happened this morning. I'm letting you know that the men who shot those two black men are being hunted down by the guardsmen. If any of you get involved in any kind of way, you will be at the mercy of the guardsmen also."

The Prince and Princess head back to the palace while Lizzes and Earl make their way to Greater Landing. When they reach Greater Landing, the people are in the streets, outraged and wanting revenge for what just happened. They are now blaming Lizzes and Earl for the incident at the coffee shop. The guardsmen are on high alert. They reach the nonprofit office, and a crowd immediately gathers. They want to know what is going to happen to the men who shot the security guards. Lizzes steps forward, announcing, "The men who shot the security guards have fled the city, and there are 20 guardsmen in pursuit to arrest them." She adds, "Rest assured, they will be caught and brought to justice." Lizzes inquires of the crowd, "Does anyone know where these two men live? We would like to meet their family and let them know that the men are in stable condition at the doctor's office in town."

Two ladies step up and inform Lizzes that they are the mothers of the men who got shot. They ask Lizzes, "When can we see our sons?" Lizzes explains, "Your sons just had surgery and are resting right now. There are four guardsmen at the doctor's office for their protection."

"If you meet me here tomorrow morning at 9 am, we will gladly take you to the doctor's office to see your sons," she adds. The ladies nod in agreement; then Lizzes and Earl enter the nonprofit. Lizzes instructs the staff to stop what they're doing. She directs, "I need you to close up the nonprofit for today and find me 50 good men. Have them meet me here tomorrow at 1 pm. Make sure they have their documentation and a clean record." The ladies close up the shop and begin to go around Greater Landing, recruiting 50 men. Earl advises Lizzes, "If you're planning on hiring 200 security guards, you may want to get this nonprofit up and running immediately." Lizzes informs Earl, "The ladies made 1200 lbs yesterday just going around town asking people about the businesses for donations. I have calculations for the nonprofit."

She goes on to say, "We need to make 15000 lbs a month to pay the ladies and the security guards. That's 4000 a week. We will fund the nonprofit for now until the nonprofit can fund itself." Lizzes also tells Earl, "Don't forget, the Royal Family is going to pay about 20000 lbs themselves for their Royal clothes being made right now, and we can expect a lot of business to come our way at the Princess ball in a couple of weeks." She adds, "I'm not worried about money. I'm worried about getting Greater Landing to a place where racism is not allowed. To do that, we are going to have to own every abandoned building here to create the business attraction that I have in mind. For now, we need to get the addresses of the abandoned buildings in Greater Landing and have the guardsmen find out who owns the buildings."

Lizzes orders two of her guardsmen, "Go around Greater Landing and get every address of abandoned buildings, then go to the book of records in town and find out who owns the buildings and how much they are worth." Lizzes and Earl head back to the palace. Meanwhile, at the palace, the King and Queen are furious at the events that happened at the coffee shop. When Lizzes and Earl arrive at the palace, they, along with the Princess and Prince, are called to the Queen's study. The Queen reveals, "I instructed the guardsmen to bring those men directly to me and the King when they are found." She also warns them, "Remember the change will also come with great pain. So don't think this is going to be easy. I want all of you to remember that. You are dismissed!!"

Meanwhile, the 20 guardsmen have gotten word from the police that the five men are on their way to Canterbury. A city near the English Channel. The five men are going to try to cross the Channel and enter France. The guardsmen are in hot pursuit and they must stop them before they cross over. The guardsmen have instructed all post offices along the way to send a telegram to delay all ships to France. They know the men have a four-hour head start on the journey by horse. If the men enter France, they will be under

France's jurisdiction. The guardsmen are riding as fast as they can to try and catch up with the five men. They slow down to cross a fifty-foot-long bridge. The bridge spans a river flowing from the English Channel. The horses stop!! They begin to try and back up on their own as if something is wrong. The guardsmen decide to dismount and walk across the bridge, but the horses will not move. Two of the guardsmen decide to go and investigate what's in front of them. As they go further onto the bridge, they realize what the horses are afraid of.

About fifteen feet of the bridge has been blown up! They couldn't see it because the bridge rises in height and declines when you cross over to the other side. The guardsmen now know they will never reach the men in time. The next bridge available to cross is a five-hour ride south. The guardsmen decide to make camp for the night and continue in the morning. They know that the ships will not be delayed an extra five hours upon their arrival, but decide to go anyway in the morning.

CHAPTER 27

PARTNERS OF ROYALTY

That evening, the guardsmen return with the town's record book and enter Lizzes' study, where she and Earl are talking. The guardsmen are filled with excitement, and Lizzes can see it. She asks the guardsmen, "What did you find out?" The guardsmen reveal, "All those buildings have been abandoned for decades, and the actual owners are the Queen's great-great-grandmother, great-great-grandfather, Princess, Prince Doris, and William Buchinham?" Lizzes is so excited that she jumps out of the chair next to Earl and her left arm hits him in the face, giving him a bloody lip. She grabs the papers out of the guardsman's hand and begins reading them. She has totally forgotten that she has given Earl a bloody lip. While Earl presses a napkin to his lip provided by the guardsman, Lizzes bolts out of the room.

Earl and the guardsmen are staring at her like she has completely lost her mind. Lizzes runs into the Queen's study, and the Queen jumps up, frightened! The Queen exclaims, "My goodness, child, what is wrong with you?" Lizzes can't even talk; she's so out of breath. While she's trying to catch her breath, she hands the papers to the Queen. The Queen begins to read the papers and falls into her rocking chair. The King inquires, "What is it?" By that time, Lizzes has caught her breath. She informs the King that he and the Queen own all the abandoned buildings in Greater Landing. The Queen exclaims, "Oh my goodness!! It says here that there are actually 23 empty buildings, and 4 of the buildings were apartment buildings." Lizzes explains, "Those buildings have been handed down to each generation that's next in line, and that would be you two."

Lizzes shows the Queen where her great-great-grandmother and grandfather had signed. Since her grandparents and two uncles have passed, the buildings are owned by the oldest grandchild, who is the Queen. At that moment, the Princess and Prince enter the study. They see the confusion on everyone's faces, and they ask, "What is wrong?" Lizzes explains the situation, and they're totally confused. The Prince questioned, "Mother, do you mean to tell me that you own all those abandoned buildings in Greater Landing?" The Queen confirms, "According to these property deeds, yes!" The Prince realizes and says, "It now makes sense. No one has tried or attempted to renovate those buildings because of the book of records. The staff probably turned everyone away when they asked or tried to pull the records on those buildings."

Lizzes immediately shares her plan with the Queen, then asks, "Queen, will you sell me those buildings?" The Queen and King burst into laughter! The Queen replies, "Now, why would I sell my daughter something that is already hers?" Lizzes immediately falls onto the Queen's lap, then begins to kiss her hands and face all over. Everyone is laughing. Then the Queen exclaims, "Young lady, will you please get up and stop kissing me!!" "My goodness!!" Lizzes gets up, then she declares, "All four of you listen to me. I'm going to sign over those buildings to all four of you. You all will work together." She then stops and questions, "Where is Earl?" The Prince answers, "We saw him heading towards the bathroom with a bloody lip." The Queen inquires, "How did he get a bloody lip?"

The Prince explains, "He told me she hit him in the mouth in her excitement." Lizzes, in disbelief, asks, "I did?" The Queen and King are shaking their heads. The Queen admonishes, "Young lady, you need to control yourself. You don't remember hitting Earl in the mouth?" Lizzes responds, "No!" The Queen remarks, "My goodness." Then Earl walks in, and Lizzes immediately starts to apologize. Earl accepts, "It's ok, I'm fine." The Queen inquires of Earl, "Are you ok?" Earl responds, "Yes, I'm ok." The Queen continues, "As I was saying, the four of you will work together to fulfill Lizzes' plan." The Queen hands Lizzes the signed papers. She informs Lizzes, “I want to see the plan on paper and exactly how it’s going to look.” Lizzes agrees, “Yes, of course, my Queen,” and begins to walk towards the Queen to give her a hug and kiss. The Queen says, “Stop, Lizzes, you have kissed and hugged me enough.” Then Lizzes looks at the King, who immediately says, “Don’t even think about it!” Everyone laughs, and the Queen orders, “You are dismissed. Please get out!” The four of them leave laughing and excited. After they leave, the King remarks, “You know Lizzes is very dominant. Even Earl backs down to her when her dominance shows up. But the Prince and Princess will not. I wonder how long it will take before they start fighting like brothers and sisters.” The Queen says with a grin, “Tomorrow.” They both begin to laugh. The Queen states, “When they start arguing, we will jump in and delegate power and responsibilities.”

Earl, Lizzes, the Princess, and the Prince all head into the living room. Lizzes muses, “I wonder if the area and the black people are the reasons why none of those buildings were developed.” The Princess asserts, “It is the sole reason. That area doesn’t have mainstream customers. The only customers are the black customers.” She questions Lizzes, “What kind of business are you trying to put into Greater Landing?” Lizzes answers, “Businesses that will attract all customers.” She adds, “Now the next step will be to find out who owns the buildings and where the black businesses are located.” The Princess inquires, “Why?” Lizzes responds, “I want to fence in that entire area and station guardsmen around certain areas inside the perimeter of the fence.” The Prince says, “I think you will have to get a permit from the city of London to do that. Then, you will have to get a grounds permit for the fencing around the perimeter of the city. You just can’t put fencing on someone else’s property.”

The Prince adds, “I will send a guardsman into the city and gather all the records on the land ownership and the other building owners in Greater Landing tomorrow morning.” Earl queries, “How many guardsmen do you think it will take to put in perimeters around Greater Landing?” Lizzes admits, “I don’t know, that city spans 12 to 15 blocks in all directions.” The Prince cautions, “Hold on! Let’s get the property deeds from the book of records and see who owns what before we start making any plans.” Lizzes pauses, then declares, “I want the entire city by all means necessary, and I’m not going to stop until I get it!!!” She gets up and walks out. Earl glances at the Princess and Prince and remarks, “She’s as stubborn as two twin jackasses!!!” They all begin to laugh as they get up and leave the living room. As the Queen and King are coming down the main hallway, they see Lizzes entering her room and slamming the door. Then they observe Earl. The Prince and the Princess come walking behind her. Earl goes into his room, and the Prince and Princess are stopped by the Queen.

The Queen inquires, “What is going on? Lizzes just walked into her room and slammed the door.” The Princess replies lightly, “Oh, nothing, just Lizzes being stubborn as two twin jackasses!” The Queen and King exchange glances as the Princess and Prince head towards their rooms. The King comments to the Queen, “Well, it did take them 30 minutes to come to a disagreement.” The Queen and King depart, shaking their heads and chuckling as they head to the bedroom. The Queen predicts, “I’ll give them a week to learn how to work together before I intervene.” At that moment, a guardsman comes in and hands the Queen a telegram from the guardsmen in hot pursuit of the five men.

CHAPTER 28

SPIES IN FRANCE

The Queen appears upset about the telegram. The telegram states, "We, the guardsmen, will not make it to Canterbury in time to stop the five men from entering France. We will arrive in Canterbury at 10 am tomorrow morning. The bridge entering Canterbury is blown up. We will be waiting for your orders to enter France silently or publicly." The Queen instructs the guardsmen to send this message: "I, the Queen, order you to investigate whether the men truly got on any one of those ships to France. Once that investigation is done, return to London. The men will be under France's jurisdiction once they enter. France will not let you arrest anyone who hasn't committed any crimes in their country. We will have to inform France of the crimes the men committed in London, and they may not arrest them. But they will stay in France. Once you get back to London, we will make plans to enter France unannounced. Once you enter France, you cannot get caught. If you get caught, you will be arrested. All government officials, when entering other countries, have to announce themselves and let that government know they are on their official business. We will see you when you get back." The guardsmen take the Queen's message back to the post office for delivery. The Queen knocks on Lizzes' door.

Lizzes opens the door. The Queen inquires, "How long will it be before you have the new guardsmen suits ready?" Lizzes explains, "The prototype is ready and is at the blacksmith for weapons installation. There are 15 suits ready for installation. The installation will be completed in a couple days." The Queen replies, "Good. I need 20 of those suits ready for training in 5 days."

Lizzes nods, "Ok, but is everything ok?" The Queen explains, "The five men will enter France sometime today, and the guardsmen will have to go into France unannounced to arrest them." Lizzes questions, "I thought we couldn't arrest anyone in France?" The Queen declares, "We can't, but we are anyway. That's why we need those suits. The guardsmen will have to blend in. They're going to need all their skill and weapons to pull this off." Lizzes acknowledges, "I understand. I will have the suits sent over to the blacksmith tomorrow." The Queen affirms, "Excellent, good night." Lizzes sits down on the bed and asks Earl, "Did you hear that?" Earl confirms, "Yes." Lizzes realizes and says, "If the guardsmen get caught, this could start a war between both countries." Earl inquires,

"How much will each suit weigh?" Lizzes answers, "Each suit will weigh About 7 lbs. The weapons are of steel, but the loading mechanism will be made out of plastic."

Earl exclaims, "Wow! This is really serious if the Queen wants those suits." Lizzes decides, "We will deal with the suit situation tomorrow. I've had enough excitement and stress for one day. Once the little Princess is asleep, meet me in the guest room!!!" She declares. Earl knows what that means and hurried to the guest room to wait for Lizzes. That evening, while the 20 guardsmen are settling in for the night, they hear voices in the distance about 50 feet north heading their way. Three of the guardsmen take their posts in the trees. While the other 15 jump into the holes they dug and cover themselves with the leaves and sticks they made for camouflage. Silently waiting, they observe three figures approaching. It's three men who are looking around with their guns pointed. The three men don't see anyone; they observe only a fire and some tents. The guardsmen's horses are 60 yards away south, being watched by the other two guardsmen. One man remarks, "It looks like an abandoned camp. Let's take everything and take it back to the town and sell it."

The guardsmen know these men are just thieves. At that moment, the guardsmen jump out of the ground with both guns pointed at the thieves. The guardsmen's faces are covered in black mud. The three men are frozen with fear. They drop their guns and immediately throw their hands up. One guardsman warns, “Don’t move, or you will die tonight.” The men are so frightened that they begin to speak French. One of the guardsmen approaches and asks,”Are you gentlemen from France?” The men reply with fear, “Yes.” The guardsman notes, “But you live in England now?” The three gentlemen confirm. The guardsmen then signal for others to come out of the trees. They come running down the trees with their ropes attached to them. The three men are scared to death!!! The head guardsman decided that they could use the men to help them when they enter France. The three men ask the guardsmen, “Are you Royal Guardsmen?” The guardsman confirms, “Yes.” the guardsmen declare, “We usually kill thieves caught in the act of stealing! But if you value your lives, you will help us on our journey.”

The guardsman explains to the three men, “We are heading into Canterbury, and we need you to come with us. There are a lot of French-speaking people there, and we don’t know the language. If you help us, we will forget about the crime you committed, and we will pay you also.” The three men agree to the guardsman’s terms. The guardsman instructs, “Meet us here at the camp tomorrow morning at 6 am.” The next morning, the three men show up. The guardsmen are now dressed in their Royal uniforms for travel. They head for Canterbury.

Meanwhile, back at the palace, Lizzes rises early and heads to the work area to check on the guardsmen's suits. The suits are ready to be sent to the blacksmith for installation. She calls for the guardsmen to come prepare the suits for delivery.

She goes back to bed. She expresses her nervousness to Earl about the Queen's plan to send the guardsmen into France unannounced. Earl explains, "The five men have not committed any crimes in France, so even if the Queen tells France, France will not do anything. So, if we want to bring the five men to justice, this is the only way. This has been said by the Queen on several occasions. Please don't question her decision." Lizzes decides to leave it alone and put her focus on the suits.

Meanwhile, at the doctor's office, both men are up and conscious. One guardsman decides to inform Lizzes about the two men's condition. But, before he leaves, the two men realize where they are and immediately try to get up and leave, but the guardsmen won't allow it. The guardsmen understand the two men are afraid of being in this part of town at the doctor's office after what happened to them. The guardsmen reassured them that they were there to protect them. Comforted, the two men relax back into their beds. After the two men calm down, the guardsmen make their way to the palace.

After entering the palace, the guardsmen proceed to the dining room to inform the family about the news. One of them tells the family that the two men have awakened and are very conscious of their surroundings. Lizzes instructs the guardsman to prepare the doctor's office for visitors. "I will be bringing their families to see them this morning," she states. The guardsmen leave to prepare the doctor's office. 20 guardsmen have finally made it to Canterbury.As they enter the city, people are staring and wondering what is going on. That 20 Royal Guardsmen have entered their city. The guardsmen stop at the Edge Water bar. The head guardsman directs five guardsmen to search all hotels for the five men. He instructs another five to check the shipyard manifest and five more to check all the bars. He keeps the other four with him and sends the three of them to go and check all the women of the night areas.

The head guardsman instructs everyone to meet back here in three hours. Before they disperse, the sheriff shows up with four of his deputies and tries to show his power. He asks the head guardsman with his hands on his hips, showing his gun and badge, "What is the reason for your presence in Canterbury?" The guardsmen get agitated! He gets off his horse, walks up to the sheriff, and states, "You, as sheriff, should know not to ever approach a guardsman and ask questions! Do you know that?" The sheriff admits, "Yes, but I was just curious about the nature of your visit to my town." This response infuriates the guardsmen. "You do know all guardsmen have jurisdiction in England over all government officials, right?" The guardsmen question. The sheriff starts to object, but the guardsman cuts him off, "No buts, hand me your badge and your gun!!" The sheriff reacts in disbelief. The sheriff protests, "Wait a minute! You can't do that! I was voted in by the people."

The guardsman asserts, "We are the people!" At that time, all of the guardsmen got off their horses and walked towards the sheriff. The deputies back up. The head guardsman demands, "Hand me your badge and your gun or be arrested!" The sheriff is angry! But knows he is outmatched and overruled. He hands the guardsmen his badge and gun, retorting, "You haven't seen the last of me!" Then, in one swift movement, the guardsman takes the sheriff to the ground. He ties up the sheriff and remarks, "Who is now bleeding from the mouth?" He inquires if the deputies had a problem with locking up the sheriff and writing a report. One of the deputies responds, "No! No problem." The guardsmen ask, "Who is second in command?" A deputy steps forward, saying, "I am." The guardsman takes off the deputy's badge and pins the sheriff's badge on him. The guardsman declares, "I grant you the role of sheriff in the name of the Queen of England and by the Royal Guardsmen." All the guardsmen affirm, "We are witnesses to the new sheriff of Canterbury."

The guardsmen tell the new sheriff to lock up the ex-sheriff and await his arrival at the sheriff's office.

The new sheriff nods and then looks at the three men with the guardsmen. He warns the guardsman, "You need to be worried about those three. They are always getting themselves into trouble." The guardsman assures, "I don't think they're going to be any trouble anytime soon." They leave the sheriff and head into the town to search for the five men.

CHAPTER 29

DOWN BUT NOT OUT

That morning, Lizzes arrives at the nonprofit building. The mother of the two wounded men awaits there. They get into Lizzes' automobile and head over to the doctor's office. The two mothers are nervous as they don't go into the city of London unless it's to work. They are wondering what the people are going to say when they see them riding with Lizzes. As they enter the city, people are staring because it's a member of the Royal Family accompanied by the Royal Guardsmen. When they arrive at the doctor's office and exit the automobile, everyone stops to stare. They stare at the two black women getting out of Lizzes automobile. They stare in a really intense way that Lizzes instructs the guardsmen to move the people along. When they enter the doctor's office, everyone stops what they are doing, and they also stare. Lizzes becomes upset. She screams at everyone looking and asks, "What are you looking at? You look like you've seen a ghost. You should see the looks on your faces." She screams! "Stop looking!" Everyone turns their gaze away. The guardsmen walk up to her and advise, "You cannot show your vulnerability to the people; you are Royalty and must be at all times." Lizzes agrees with the guardsmen. She walks up to a nurse and informs, "These are the two men's mothers. They would like to see their sons." The nurse leads the mothers to their sons, who are in the same room. When the two men see their mothers, they begin to cry. They share with their mothers that they do not want this job. They request their mothers to inform the Duchess of their decision to decline the jobs.

The mothers advise their sons that they will have to tell her themselves and that they should take some time to think about their decisions. The mothers warn their sons that if they quit now, then they will always give up when things get hard. They urge their sons, "Get some rest, and we will come to get you in a couple days." The two mothers head back out into the waiting area where Lizzes is. Lizzes asks the mothers, "How are the two men doing?" The mothers explain, "They are both traumatized and want to quit their jobs. They're afraid." Lizzes responds, "Well, I can't blame them for feeling that way. They almost died!!!" The mothers request Lizzes to give them some time to heal. They leave the doctor's office and return to Greater Landing. Upon entering Greater Landing, the guardsmen notice something unusual. They see two white men dressed very nicely at the entrance of the nonprofit. The head guardsman directs two guards to go and see what the two white men are doing at the nonprofit while the rest escort the two mothers home with Lizzes.

The two guardsmen arrive at the nonprofit and ask the two white men, "What business do you have here?" The white men retort, "This is our building, and we just stop by to see what business is being conducted here." The guardsmen inform the two men that Duchess Lizzes owns the nonprofit and inquire if they have any questions for her. The two men ignore what the guardsmen just said and tell them to inform the Duchess that the rent of this building will be increasing. The guardsman gets off from his horse and walks up to the two men, an inch from both of their faces. He states, "We guardsmen don't like to be disrespected! I just told you if you have any questions to ask the Duchess, but you continued to ignore us and ask us to tell the Duchess your information."

He goes on to say, "It's ok. The duchess owns 23 other buildings in Greater Landing, and this will be the last month here." The two white men question, "Does the Duchess have documentation on those buildings? We have been trying for years to get documentation but with no luck."

The guardsman confirms, "Yes," and wishes them a nice day. The guardsmen enter the nonprofit and ask the ladies, "Are you okay?" The ladies affirm, "Yes, they didn't even come in. They just stayed outside looking at the building." The guardsman decides to stay with the ladies until Lizzes arrives. He heads into the lounge area and takes a seat. Meanwhile, Lizzes drops off the two mothers and assures them she will return in two days to take them to see their sons again. Lizzes and the guardsmen depart and head towards the nonprofit office.

Once they arrive, the guardsmen inform Lizzes about the two white men. Lizzes becomes very angry and instructs one of the guardsmen to find the two white men and inform them that she wants to meet them tomorrow at 11 am. Lizzes checks on the ladies and requests them to inform the security guards to meet her here tomorrow at 9 am. The guardsmen leave to find the men. Lizzes heads back to the palace.

Meanwhile, back in Canterbury, five of the guardsmen go into a bar called Seven Seas. The bar was decorated with various different types of marine life. The lead guardsman walks up to the bar and inquires about the bartender's name. The bartender says, "Raymond." Raymond inquires, "What brings the famous Royal Guardsmen to the town of Canterbury?" The guardsman hands the bartender, who is dressed in a long gray shirt with a black server apron on, a flyer with the five men's pictures on it. The guardsmen question, "Have you seen these men in town?" The bartender responds, "Yes! I saw them yesterday; they were heading to the shipyard. They had one drink and were in a hurry." Raymond informed the guardsmen that they were there having a drink with the sheriff.

All the guardsmen look at each other. Raymond continues, " I think the sheriff is related to two of the gentlemen." The guardsmen express their thanks and exit the bar in a hurry. The guardsmen now realize why the sheriff approached them when they first entered town. The sheriff was trying to stall the guardsmen. The sheriff was buying time for the five men to reach the shipyard. The guardsmen suspect that the five men haven't left yet and are still at the shipyard.

The five guardsmen race to the sheriff's office to confront the former sheriff. The guardsmen reach the sheriff's office. One of the guardsmen sends up a yellow smoke signal to caution the other guardsmen to be on alert. The guardsmen burst into the sheriff's office to confront the former sheriff. The deputy on duty is surprised and frightened. He's never seen guardsmen but has heard about them. The guardsmen don't recognize the deputy. One of the guardsmen inquires of the deputy, "Where is the former sheriff? He's supposed to be locked up." The deputy admits, "The former sheriff was never brought back here, and I don't know where he is." The guardsmen exchange looks again, realizing they have been deceived. They rush back outside and send out a red smoke signal, instructing all the guardsmen to stop what they're doing, be on high alert, and meet where the red smoke is being signaled from.

◆◆◆

CHAPTER 30

AMBUSHED IN CANTERBURY

Meanwhile, at the Bortsworth Hotel, the five guardsmen see the red and yellow smoke. They leave the hotel and head towards the smoke. Meanwhile, the other five guardsmen at the Women of the Night building are questioning the ladies about the five men. The ladies attempt to seduce the guardsmen and try to get them to go upstairs with them. The guardsmen decline their offers, but the ladies refuse to take no for an answer. Some of the ladies block the exits and lock the doors. The guardsmen become angry and aggressive at the ladies' approach, and sense that something isn't right. All five guardsmen go into protective mode, and at the same time, a bomb enters the building with red smoke.

The inside of the building is filled with red smoke, causing everyone to cough as they exit from both upstairs and downstairs. The guardsmen, undetected, had already made their way outside and bombed the two-block area with red smoke. Now, everyone in that area is coughing and trying to escape the red smoke. The five guardsmen, unnoticed, climbed their way to the top of the building and are now watching everyone, as the smoke has no effect on them. Guardsmen are positioned on each side at the top of the building. The guardsmen on the building's south side notice six men running out from the back of the building. One of the guardsmen recognizes all the men, including the former sheriff. They are the newly elected sheriff and the four deputies. The guardsmen are wondering why the sheriff isn't locked up. The guardsmen signal for the other guardsmen. They watch as the sheriff, the former sheriff, and the four deputies move toward clear air.

The head guardsman signals two guardsmen to jump into action and capture the men for questioning. The two guardsmen jump off the two-story building, land on their feet, and begin to run after the men. They throw their ropes into a tree and begin climbing the tree. They then move from branch to branch. The guardsmen in the trees finally reach clear air and catch up to the men. The two guardsmen are 20 feet above the men, and then they jump out of the tree with blue bombs of smoke. None of the men can see anything. All that can be heard is a lot of screaming and shouting. The men are scared to death as they are being attacked by the guardsmen who are moving at a blinding speed. The five men have no clue about what's going on. At the same time, the two guardsmen start spinning really fast with their coat jackets flung open. When they turn, the force of their movements pushes the blue smoke further into the air. As the smoke clears, the five men, who are now in bull rope from their feet to hands, which are now tied behind their backs, look up and see the two guardsmen. They are stunned as the two guardsmen take them down so quickly that they have no chance to react. Now, there's blue, yellow, and red smoke everywhere ascending into the sky. The other three guardsmen jump off the two-story building, land on their feet, and run toward the other two guardsmen. They untie the men's feet and take them back to the jail.

The newly appointed sheriff inquires about the guardsmen, "What is going on? Why are we tied up?" The guardsmen remain silent. Then one of the deputies exclaims, "I told you to lock up the former sheriff, but you wouldn't listen. That's the only reason I can think of why we're tied up." The men now argue among themselves, asserting, "I told you we should have locked up the sheriff." The guardsmen say nothing and just continue to walk them towards the sheriff's office. Meanwhile, the five guardsmen who were at the shipyard have now reached the sheriff's office and met the other five guardsmen from the bar. One of the guardsmen informs the lead guardsman, "The former sheriff isn't locked up, and he is also related to two of the five men we are looking for, and they still could be at the shipyard." The lead guardsman orders, "Four of you stay alert outside until the other five guardsmen show up. The rest of you stay inside." The lead guardsman greets the deputy inside. He begins to ask him questions. He asks the deputy, "How long have you been on duty?" The deputy answers, "Since this morning."

The lead guardsman questions, "Did four deputies and a new sheriff ever show up with the former sheriff who is supposed to be locked up?" The deputy reacts, "What are you talking about? There is a new sheriff. Really! I don't know anything about that. No one has shown up here. It's just been me. I was supposed to be relieved two hours ago." Just then, the five guardsmen show up with the four deputies and the former sheriff." He then asks, "What in the hell is going on here?" The lead guardsman declares, "We are about to find out!!" The lead guardsman instructs the guardsmen to untie the men. He orders the deputy to lock all the men up except for the former sheriff. The deputy follows the lead guardsman's orders.

As the deputy locks up each man, he questions the men, "What is going on? What did you guys do?" The men reply, "We will tell you later, not now." The lead guardsman directs ten guardsmen to go outside and secure the perimeter of the sheriff's office. A crowd has gathered because they have watched the guardsmen escort all five men, including the former sheriff, in handcuffs to the sheriff's office. He instructs the three thieves to go to the bar and wait for them there. The lead guardsman inquires of the deputy if he has locked up all the men. The deputy confirms, "Yes, but can you please explain to me what is going on here?" The lead guardsman responds, “Yes! But not now. For now, I am relieving you of your duties for tonight. We will see you in the morning.” The deputy looks around at the guardsmen. Then he looks at the former sheriff and leaves. The lead guardsman sets the former sheriff in a chair in the middle of the room, and all nine guardsmen surround him. The head guardsman unties the former sheriff. He asks, “Where are the five men headed when they reach France?” The former sheriff states, “I’m not telling you anything.” The head guardsman nods by saying, “OK.” He takes a piece of paper from the sheriff’s desk and then draws a picture of the former sheriff on it.

He writes, “People of Canterbury, we, the guardsmen, have stripped your sheriff off his title for disrespecting a guardsman, and now he is being locked up for conspiracy of attempted murder. He has refused to cooperate with the guardsmen in capturing five men who have fled London to seek asylum in France for attempted murder. Until the former sheriff cooperates with the guardsmen, the city of Canterbury will be shut down until further notice, starting immediately.”

The guardsmen read the statement out loud to the former sheriff. The former sheriff protests to the guardsman, “You’re not going to print that!” The lead guardsman hands the paper to a guardsman and instructs him to go to the print shop and have 1000 copies printed up. Seeing the guardsmen’s seriousness, the sheriff relents, “Ok, ok, I’ll tell you what you want to know.” The guardsman inquires of the former sheriff, "Where are the five men heading to France?" The sheriff replies, "Paris." The lead guardsman then questions, "What ship are they on?" The former sheriff responds, "The Bounded Blue."

The guardsman inquires, "What's the address the five men will be staying at?" The former sheriff admits, "I don't know the address, but they will be staying at Hotel Bordeaux." The guardsman accepts, "Ok, stay right here." The lead guardsman goes to the place where the four deputies and sheriff are locked up. The lead guardsman asks the sheriff, "Do you know why you are locked up?" The sheriff admits, "Yeah, we didn't lock up the former sheriff, and we disobeyed a direct order from a guardsman." The head guardsman confirms, "Correct, but did you also know that the former sheriff was helping five men who are up for attempted murder in London who we are chasing, escape to France?" The sheriff and the four deputies are utterly shocked!! The sheriff explains, "We knew the five men, and two of them are related to the former sheriff, but we didn't know all that. We just thought they were passing through, and I didn't want them to see the former sheriff locked up while his family was visiting. So, the former sheriff asked me if it was ok to take him to jail later after he spent some time with his family."

The guardsman questions the sheriff, "What is your connection to the former sheriff? He must mean something to you for you to disobey a direct order from a guardsman, knowing the consequences if you did?" The sheriff reveals, "He is the only father I've ever known since I was five years old. He has a wife and three children, not including me." He adds, "So what's next for us?" The guardsman looks at all the men locked up and states, "I believe that you didn't know the seriousness of the situation, so I'm gonna release you. But you, sheriff, will be suspended for one week without pay for disobeying a direct order from the guardsman." One of the deputies whispers to another, "Man, they have more power than the highest-ranking government officials in England, including the military." The guardsmen release all the men. The sheriff questions, "What about my father? He's nearing retirement, and I really don't want him to go out like this."

The guardsmen propose, "You know what, if he writes a letter to the Queen of England admitting what he did and apologizing for his actions, I will leave his fate up to you." The sheriff responds, "Agreed." They walk back into the holding area where the former sheriff is. The sheriff informs the former sheriff, his father, "If you write a letter to the Queen of England apologizing for your actions and admitting what you have done, then your fate will be in my hands." The sheriff agrees to the terms. The guardsman declares, "Ok, when you write the letter, give it to me, and I will deliver it myself." The former sheriff, overwhelmed with relief and joy, expresses his gratitude, "Thank you!! I will write it tonight when I get home." Then, the sheriff surprises everyone, including the guardsmen. He tells the former sheriff, "No, you won't be writing it from home. You will be writing it from a jail cell tonight."

The former sheriff appears discouraged but concedes, "You are right. I put you guys through a lot today and it's only fair that I agree to your terms." The sheriff states, "I will inform Mother about your actions and let her know you're fine." The head guardsman looks at the sheriff and gives him a couple of nods. The sheriff gets a notepad and a pen from the desk and escorts the former sheriff, his father to his jail cell. He instructs two of his deputies to stay on duty until tomorrow morning. The head guardsman informs the sheriff, "Our time is up here. We will be heading back tomorrow morning." The head guardsman instructs all the guardsmen to head to the hotel and call it a night. The guardsmen request the sheriff to go to the bar, find the three thieves, and inform them that we will be leaving in the morning, but we will be back in one month. The head guardsman adds, "Give the thieves this money and tell them to stay out of trouble," the sheriff agrees. The guardsmen arrive at the hotel and inform the hotel clerk that they want an entire floor.

The clerk explains, "The 3rd has reservations for six guests checking in today, but they are not here." The head guardsman declares, "Move them, and we want the entire floor." The clerk acknowledges, "Ok." The head guardsman instructs, "Also, have your security on standby at every exit and entrance on the 3rd floor."

The clerk responds, "As you wish. Should I charge this to the Queen's account?" The guardsman affirms, "Yes." Then he requests, "Have our horses taken to the barn and taken care of for tonight, and we will see you in the morning."

"Oh, lock down the hotel for tonight. No one gets in or out after your last guest is checked in," He adds. The clerk agrees, "Ok, good night." That night, the head guardsman writes a telegram to the Queen, "Your Majesty, we have information on where the five men will be staying in France. We've gathered lots of information and will be returning to London as soon as possible. We will arrive in London in three days."

◆◆◆

CHAPTER 31

DRESSED TO KILL

The next morning at breakfast, the Queen receives a telegram from the guardsman. She reads it and turns to Lizzes. Lizzes inquires, "What is it, my Queen?" The Queen reports, "The 20 guardsmen have located the whereabouts of the five men. Unfortunately, the five men have boarded a ship and are heading to France." She then asks Lizzes, "What is the progress on the 20 new suits?" Lizzes responds, "The installation should be completed this morning." The Queen directs the guardsman on duty, "Go and check on the suits and bring them back to the palace." She then states, "Lizzes, you and your coworkers design the suits, so it's only fair that you and the ladies set up a training class for the 20 guardsmen." Lizzes agrees, "Ok, we will have a training class ready in five days." The Queen counters, "You have three. The 20 guardsmen will arrive in three days, and I want them trained by the end of the month."

Lizzes affirms, “Yes, your Majesty.” After breakfast, Lizzes, Earl, the Prince, and the Princess head out to the coffee shop. When they arrive at the coffee shop, they spot two white men waiting for Lizzes inside. The two men see that the Duchess has brought backup. The Royal Family enters the coffee shop and makes their way to their table. They walk past the two men without saying a word. Lizzes knows the two men are very disrespectful, so she’s going to talk to them on her time, not theirs.

The two men are very excited to talk to the Duchess about the buildings owned by the Royal Family, so after being ignored for about twenty minutes, they decide to make their move. They get up, approach the Royal Family, and try to walk past the guardsmen. Two guardsmen stop both of them, throw them up against the wall, and begin to pat them down for weapons. The two men demand, “What is the meaning of this? Do you know who we are? We are members of one of the richest families in England, the Dweet Family.” The guardsman replies, “I don’t care who you are. You don’t ever walk past a guardsman to get to the Royal Family.” After patting them down, he instructs the two men to stand there. As the two men are standing, the Royal Family isn’t giving them any of their attention. After five minutes, Lizzes signals the guardsmen to let the two men pass. The two men immediately begin to talk, but they don’t even acknowledge the Royal Family.

The two men inquire, "We heard you have deeds to the 23 abandoned buildings. May we see them?" The Royal Family gets very upset, and before Lizzes can say anything, the head guardsman steps in. He instructs the two men to step back. The two men ask, "What is the problem?" The guardsman explains to the men, "You didn't acknowledge the Royal Family, and that's very disrespectful. So, this is what's going to happen. The black businesses that are in your buildings in Greater Landing will be moving out into the Royal families' buildings. Their leases will be up in two months, some in one month. You will no longer charge them double the rent." The two men protest, "Wait a minute, we have 21 leases in that town." The guardsman states, "Not anymore."

At that moment, Lizzes hands the guardsman a letter. She whispers something to the guardsman. The guardsman tells the two men, "Here is a cheque for all the remaining leases that the business owners owe you. The business owners have signed new leases with the royal families and are now under the protection of the guardsmen." The guardsman hands the cheque to the two men and informs them, "Your services are no longer needed!!!" The two men become angry. They exclaim to the Royal Family, "You cannot do this to us!!" The guardsman steps in again and this time more forcefully. He closes in on the two men's faces and warns, "Watch what you say next cause if you say the wrong thing, it will be very bad for you." The two men back away in fear and decide that it isn't a good idea to anger the guardsmen.

They decide to leave but are highly upset. The family asks Lizzes, "Did you know that those two men were that disrespectful?" Lizzes confirms, "Yes, that's why I had the guardsmen get the balances and copies of all the leases. For years, those two men have been charging double and sometimes triple rent. That's over now." She continues, "Now I will send them an offer for the sale of their buildings after the black business owners' leases are up and they move out."

As the Royal Family leaves the coffee shop, Lizzes tells the head guards to take two guardsmen and head to Greater Landing to watch over the black-owned business. She expresses her concern to the guardsmen that she has a bad feeling about those two men. The Royal Family then returns to the palace. Once they reach the palace, they see one of the guardsmen is back from a blacksmith with the suits. Lizzes gets very excited cause she has a big surprise for everyone. The guardsmen bring the suits inside into the living room. Lizzes instructs one of the guardsmen to go find the King and Queen. Everyone is now in the living room, including three guardsmen and Lizzes' coworkers. Lizzes asks the three ladies, her coworkers, to come to the front with her.

Lizzes announces, "We have a big surprise for you." She explains, "Not only do we have the suits, but…" Lizzes pulls out the first suit and explains what each color represents. It's a light brown suit, the color of sand. Then she reveals the next suit, which is dark and light blue, the colors of water. She displays the next suit, which is dark orange and red, the colors of fire. She presents the fourth suit, and it's white, which signifies the clouds. The Queen and the rest of the family are loving the color of the suits and are very excited about it. The Queen requests, "Explain to me what each element will mean when it comes to the guardsmen."

Lizzes explains, "Well, when you see the white guardsmen, they represent silence and swiftness. The white guardsmen can strike without you knowing it. You will never see it coming. The dark and light blue guardsmen strike like a hurricane and come with destructive category forces. The light brown guardsmen represent camouflage, and they are able to blend in anywhere. They could be sitting next to you, and you would never know it." She continues, "The red and orange guardsmen, well, when they are called upon, it means someone in a country has done something threatening to England or to one of our allies or family members. Then, the red and orange guardsmen will come with fire and brimstone."

The Royals have a look of disbelief on their faces. They can't believe how Lizzes' brain works! Lizzes then asks one of her coworkers, Vivian, to go to the dressing room and put on the woman's suit. Vivian comes out wearing the suit, which, to everyone's surprise, looks like a regular Dress. Lizzes instructs Vivian to pull the two strings located underneath the armpits of the dress. Vivian pulls the two strings, and to everyone's surprise, the dress transforms into a pantsuit for a woman. Lizzes directs Vivian to activate and load the weapon's chamber and tells the two guardsmen to pay attention cause all suits' weapons are activated and loaded the same way, each containing 100 steel darts. Vivian takes her right hand and touches her left shoulder until she hears a click. This loads the weapon's chamber on the left side of the suit. Then Vivian uses her left hand to touch her right shoulder until a click is heard, and this activates the weapon's chamber on the right side of the suit.

Lizzes instructs Vivian to deactivate the weapon chambers on each side of the suit by touching each shoulder in the same manner. Lizzes directs everyone to follow her into the work area and asks the two guardsmen to bring all the suits there. Once everyone gathers in the work area, they see standing dummies made out of pillows in the south corner. Lizzes requests everyone to stand back and instructs Vivian to activate the weapon's chambers.

She then advises the guardsmen to pay close attention. Lizzes tells Vivian to strike the center dummy first. Vivian stretches out her right arm. Her arm is pointing straight at the center dummy. Vivian hears a click. She rotates her body 180 degrees, keeping her arm straight. When she turns back around with a little speed, the suit takes over, remembers the target, and stops Vivian when her arm points at the target. Then, it fired a steel dart at the dummy from the top end of the sleeve jacket. The dart hit the dummy with such force that it went through the pillow of the wood and pierced a hole in the rock wall. Everyone is stunned, including the guardsmen and Lizzes. Nobody expected that a 4-inch steel dart weighing no more than two or three ounces could do so much damage. Lizzes then instructs Vivian to turn 90 degrees and aim at all three dummies. Vivian loads the weapon's chamber. She points at all three dummies with her right arm until she hears a click at each dummy she points at. She turns 90 degrees and turns back around with a little speed, and the suit takes over and fires one dart at the first dummy it locks onto, and without pointing at any of the other dummies, it fires two darts at others. But this time, the darts only pierce halfway through the wood of the dummies.

The family is in awe!! Lizzes is puzzled, and so is Vivian because the two darts that hit the center dummy and the dummy to its left were fired at an angle and then curved to hit the dummies'center mass with the same force. Everyone is in shock!!! The Royal Family is in total disbelief at what they're seeing, and so is Vivian!! Lizzes now tells Vivian to use the hat. Vivian, having designed the hat herself, knows exactly what it can do. She touches the tip of the hat with her thumb and index finger. She tips her hat in the direction of the dummy and hears a click. She turns 90 degrees to the right, takes the hat off, and throws it. This action activates the chamber of the weapon, and the edges around the hat transform from cotton material to a sharp one, like a knife. The hat makes a circular motion and heads right at the head of the dummy and cuts the head off. The hat returns to Vivian, but within 10 feet of the suit, it deactivates, and Vivian catches it. The entire room is stunned and shocked, including Lizzes and Vivian.

Lizzes instructs Vivian to open the suit jacket. Inside the suit jacket, around the entire base of the perimeter, there are four compartments designed for small handguns. The Queen asks, "Where are the guns?" Lizzes replies, "They are being specially made at the blacksmith. Each gun will weigh about 8 ounces and will be 4 inches in length and 2 inches wide and match the color of each suit." Lizzes then instructs Vivian to activate the coat's weapon's chamber. Vivian pulls down on the bottom ends of the coat on the left and right sides, like she's straightening out her coat. She hears and feels a click. She points to the inside bottom edges of the coat at the left and the right dummies. She hears and feels another click, and the coat locks onto its target. Vivian bends down, jumps in the air, and executes a 360 turn. The bottom part of the coat opens up in mid-turn and shoots four darts, hitting two dummies on the left and right before Vivian can land on her feet. Lizzes and the rest of the family, including Josephine and Alicia, all duck down.

The Queen exclaims, "My Goodness!!! That was scary!!!" "Yes, that was!!" agrees the King. The Queen inquires of Lizzes, "Who else besides you and these ladies has the blueprints to these designs?" Lizzes responds, "No one except the blacksmith." The Queen instructs Lizzes, "Put guardsmen around the blacksmith and his family 24 hours a day. We don't want anything to happen to him or these designs to get into the wrong hands." Lizzes signals to the guardsmen to do what the Queen just asked. The Queen states, "We need 20 brown suits ready in 3 days for the 20 guardsmen coming back from Canterbury." Lizzes replies, "Ok, but we have 16 brown suits ready. We have 20 extra suits in the closet ready for weapons installation. We just have to take the suits to the blacksmith." She adds, "The other colored suits are for future events." Everyone starts to leave, and then Lizzes says, "Hold up. I have one more weapon to show you." She instructs Vivian to stand on her tiptoes. Vivian does. She feels and hears the click in both boots.

Lizzes directs, "Now turn in the direction of the middle dummy." She directs Vivian to kick her right leg forward like she is trying to kick someone. Vivian kicks out her leg, and a dart comes out of the bottom of the boot, striking the dummy in the knee area. Then Lizzes tells Vivian to point both boots in the direction of all three dummies. Vivian does. Then Lizzes instructs her to kick both legs one at a time at any dummy. Vivian kicks both legs at the right-side dummy. Darts come out of the bottom of both boots and strike all three dummies in the same spot on each. Lizzes is so amazed that she exclaims something, which Earl and the Queen immediately shut down. She says, “I’m so excited I’m going to go train as a guardsman.” Earl retorts, “When hell freezes over,” the Queen adds, “Exactly! It’s not going to happen, so forget about it right now. Do you understand, young lady?” Lizzes responds with a frown, “Yes, I understand.” The Queen and King shake their head at Lizzes because they can’t believe she just said that.

Lizzes announces, “All suits come with the same color smoke bombs. That’s the end of the presentation.” The Queen approves, “Good! We need to start manufacturing 20 suits a week. Do whatever it takes to get it done.” She directs the guardsmen, “Tomorrow, go and ask the blacksmith what he needs to get this done.” The Queen instructs Lizzes and the ladies to prepare their training class for the 20 guardsmen arriving in 3 days. They head back into the living room. Suddenly, a guardsman comes in with a telegram for Lizzes. It reads, “We, the guardsmen, have located the 3 Chinese men and are on our way back to London with them. We are saying our goodbyes to the head officials of Bordeaux, and We will arrive in 4 days.” Lizzes is all smiles.

The Queen questions, “What is it.” Lizzes explains, “The last piece of the guardsmen suit training, the guardsmen are bringing back three Chinese men who are masters of kung fu.” The Prince asks, “Lizzes, you are going to combine those suits with martial arts?" Lizzes confirms, "Exactly!! They will be a deadly fighting machine and keepers of the peace." The Queen declares, "That's it. I'm tired. I'm going to take a nap. I've seen enough this morning." She instructs Lizzes to send the ladies home for the rest of the day and prepare for tomorrow. The Queen heads to her bedroom along with the King. The Princess whispers into Lizzes' ear, "I want one of those suits made especially for me." Lizzes replies, "I do, too!"

◆◆◆

CHAPTER 32

CLASS IS IN SESSION

After waking from her nap, the Queen heads toward the dining room for lunch, which starts in 30 minutes, but the Queen likes to arrive early. She overhears Lizzes, the butler, and the Queen's two personal servants speaking the language of her great-great-grandmother. She walks in, and everyone gets quiet. The Queen says, "No, no, keep going. I just want to hear the language spoken." Lizzes responds, "Ok." Lizzes then changes subject and asks the two Queen's servants to show the Queen what they've learned. The two servants begin to have a conversation.

After they are done, Lizzes tells them to explain to the Queen what they said. The two servants inform the Queen, "After this class, we need to hurry and help to get the lunch ready. After lunch we will have to go and do laundry and then help with dinner." The Queen is amazed by how much they've learned. Then the butler says to Lizzes in that language, "They are right. We have to go and prepare lunch.

Can we continue tomorrow?" Lizzes agrees, "Yes." The Queen asks the butler, "What did you say?" The butler replies, "I said we have to go and get lunch ready. Can we continue tomorrow?" The Queen loves it. Lizzes informs the butler and the two servants, "We will continue in the morning." After the butler and the Queen's two servants leave, the Queen tells Lizzes that she wants to talk to her. Lizzes says, "Ok," and sits back down. The Queen says to Lizzes, "I can see your vision, but that's not what I want to talk to you about. I want to know what in your past makes you think the way you do."

Lizzes explains, "Well, I've seen slavery, I continue to see racism towards people because of the color of their skin, I see hatred towards a person of color. I see poverty in the people of color that I don't see in the white race. I see people, just because of the color of their skin, have laws made just to keep them oppressed. I see colored people living in a segregated area and treated like low-class citizens by governments who want to keep them low-class citizens. I see the white race get jobs that the black race can't get because of the color of their skin. I see the military has no black people, I see that there are also no black people in the Royal guardsmen, I see black people getting shot just because of the color of their skin. I hate it, and I want to change that as much as possible."

The Queen affirms, "You are only 21 years old, but you have an old soul. I'm sorry that you had to witness all of that at such a young age. It's truly wrong what's happened to black people, and is still happening even after slavery. I can see the driving force and what's pushing you to change it." Lizzes responds, "There will always be racism towards another race because of the color of their skin, but I can only change what I can change. I want people of color to have the same opportunities as other races." The Queen asserts, "I have no doubt that you are going to change the world, but it won't be easy. Just remember that. I can see your vision, and that's why I haven't interfered with any of your ideas." Lizzes responds, "Thank you. That means a lot coming from you. I can't change the world, but I can create places where there is no racism or poverty, and no people are treated unfairly because of the color of their skin."

The Queen inquires, "How will you create places?" Lizzes explains, "I can buy land and create a town or city where racism and unfair treatment because of the skin color is not allowed." The Queen asks, "Is that your goal? To buy land and to build cities?" Lizzes affirms, "Yes! World cities all over the planet. It's a dream that I've had." The Queen notes, "That will cost a lot of money." Lizzes acknowledges, "I know, but that's in the future, maybe a decade away." The Queen comments, "You have a lot in your head for a 21-year-old. I would advise you to take your time and plan out everything. If you don't, you will be all over the place." She then asks, "I haven't heard you say anything about you or Earl's parents, but we can talk about that another day."

Lizzes notes, “Speaking of our parents, after the Princess’ ball and Darlene’s return, Earl and I will travel back home to visit our families.” The Queen directs, “When you go, make sure you take the Prince and Princess with you. They really need to get out of the palace.” Lizzes agrees, “That’s not a bad idea. I will ask them if they want to go.” The Queen instructs, “No! Let me know when you are going, and I will make sure they go with you. If you ask them, they will say no! I know those two.” The Queen observes, “I see you are making changes to Greater Landing. What is your plan for that part of town?” Lizzes tells the Queen, “I plan to turn that city into a tourist attraction, but there will be no racism or racist allowed inside that city. The guardsmen will force that ruling. They will also surround the city and be its protectors. That will be the first city under guardsmen’s control. So, anyone who doesn’t want to abide by these rules will not be allowed into the city.”

The Queen exclaims, “All of your thoughts are from racism!! That’s your driving force!!” Lizzes explains, “I don’t know why I feel this way, but I just want a place where that type of behavior isn’t welcome. I hate it with a passion.” The Queen remarks, “21 years old, huh!!” Lizzes smiles and shares, “In 2 years, Greater Landing will be the first example of this plan, but it starts with the guardsmen. Everything thing starts and ends with the guardsmen.” She continues, “In order for this plan to work. The guardsmen have to be the most respected and feared organization in the world.” The

Queen reflects, "We all have done wrong and learned from our wrongdoings. But with you, it's like you have been through a lot and learned from what you have been through when actually you really haven't been through anything yet!!! It's like you're living someone else's life." Lizzes admits, "I've actually felt like I'm doing that for someone else's dreams on many occasions." The Queen suggests, "Well, let's continue this talk some other time. Let's go and have lunch."

During lunch, the Prince says to the Queen and King, "Mom, Dad, I think Lizzes and my wife are somehow going to make one of those suits for themselves secretly." Lizzes and the Princess are frozen stiff!! The Queen asserts, "What, how do you know this?" The Prince explains, "Well, I overheard my wife tell Lizzes that she wanted one of those suits for herself, and Lizzes said, I know me too." Earl is visibly upset! The Queen commands, "Listen, both of you right now. This will be the last time I say this! If I catch either of you wearing or participating in any training with those suits or guardsmen, I will put a stop to everything! Are we clear?" The two women reply, "Yes, ma'am." Both of the women give the Prince a stern look! Then the Queen shoots back at the Prince, "And you, stop telling on your wife!! Take her to a room or somewhere privately and discuss the situation!" The Prince responds, "Yes, ma'am!!" Then Queen orders, "Both of you, stop staring at him!!"

The Queen and King rise from the table and warn, "You four better behave!!"

Earl protests, "But Your Majesty, I haven't done or said anything." The Queen asks, "Are you married to your wife?" Earl responds, "Yes, ma'am." The Queen declares, "Well, whatever she does, you also do. Whatever you do, she also does!" The Queen leaves the room. The King, smiling and laughing, looks at all four of them and remarks, "You children better watch yourself, especially you two ladies. She can put a stop to everything you are trying to do." He smiles and begins to walk out of the room. He stops, turns around, and says to the Prince, "Oh yeah, let me know how that couch feels to sleep on. I'm pretty sure you will be on it tonight." He exits while laughing. After the King leaves, Earl retorts to the Prince, "See what you did. You got all of us in trouble by running your mouth!"

The Prince exclaims, "Aw, shut up, you would have done the same thing." Earl dismisses with the Prince, "Whatever!" The Princess demands, "Both of you, just stop!!" She warns the Prince, "I will deal with you later!" The Prince apologizes, "I'm sorry, it won't happen again." The Princess asserts, "Oh, I know it won't." Earl begins to laugh and offers, "I have extra pillows for the couch if you want them." Lizzes snaps at Earl, "Will you shut up!!" The Prince adds, "Yeah, just shut up!!" Earl, still laughing, tells Lizzes, "He started it all." The Princess declares, "Listen, from now on, we discuss all issues together and come to a conclusion and then take it to the Queen."

"Yes," agrees Lizzes, "And no more snitching to the Queen," while looking at the Prince. The Prince reiterates, "I said I was sorry!" The Princess retorts, "You're not sorry yet, but you will be!!"

Earl starts laughing!! Lizzes gives Earl a stern look and asks, "Would you like to sleep in the guest room again?" Earl insists, "No!" Lizzes commands, "Well, then shut your mouth!!" The two ladies get up and leave the dining table while Earl and the Prince finish their lunch. Earl remarks, "See what snitching will do." The Prince retorts, "Aw, shut up! And keep your voice down before they hear you." Just then, the ladies walk back in. They command Earl and the Prince, "Get up from the table. You're done!" The gentlemen protest, "We're not finished yet!" And both ladies give them a stare. They both relent, "I'm coming!" And leave the dining room table with both ladies arguing, "You guys act like two big, grown kids." Earl starts to object, but Lizzes cuts him off, "No buts, just be quiet!!" The two men look at each other with a knowing stare as if to say, "See what you did!!"

After a quick nap with Princess Lizzie, Earl, Lizzes, the Princess, and the Prince decide to take a ride into London. They dress up in their polo uniforms. They notice that the streets are clean, and the horses are in the back of the buildings on a new horse trail. Lizzes observes many street cleaners keeping horse waste off the streets. As they ride by the coffee shop, Lizzes notices a homeless man at the side door. She instructs her driver to stop. She gets out of her automobile. The rest of the Royal Family follows her. She walks up to the homeless man. She interrupts, “Excuse me, sir.” The gentleman looks up and recognizes the Royal Family. He stands up and bows to them. Lizzes asks, “Sir, how are you doing? We have never seen you or any homeless person in the city. You are usually in the park.”

The homeless man replies, “We are not doing so well. I’m here at the side door of the coffee shop waiting for the manager to bring out leftover food from lunch so I can take it back and share it with the homeless in the park.” Just then, a deputy shows up and tells the homeless man to beat it, “Get back to the park.” Lizzes looks at the guardsmen. The guardsmen immediately instruct the deputy to stand down and leave the homeless guy alone. The deputy looks at the Royal Family, acknowledges them, and departs. The homeless man appreciates them and tells the Royal Family, “Thank you.” Lizzes asserts, “You must be very hungry to venture into the city. I thought the restaurants, after each shift, bring their leftovers to the park for the homeless.” The homeless man explains, “They usually do, but for the last three days, they have not brought anything, and the homeless people are afraid to come into the city." Lizzes asks, "What is your name?"

The homeless man responds, "Valiant George." He goes on to say, "I came to London from Manchester with my girlfriend, but she ran off with another man and took all the money we saved up two months ago. I was going to make my way back home, but so many homeless people here need help, and I just couldn't leave them. So, I decided to stay with them."

The Royal Family is saddened by what Valiant just told them. Lizzes says, "You risk your own well-being for other people." The Princess adds, "God brought you here and put you through what you went through so that you could help the homeless." Valiant begins to cry and says, "I've never looked at it like that. I just thought God was punishing me for something I did wrong." Lizzes affirms, "Sometimes God has to put us through hardships just so he can use and put us where he wants us. You're right where you are supposed to be." Lizzes instructs the guardsmen to go into all the restaurants and buy food for all the homeless people. Lizzes asks Valiant, "How many homeless people are in the park?" He replies, "Right now, about 30, but in the evening, it's around 60 of us." Lizzes directs the guardsmen to hurry and buy food and drinks for all the homeless. She informs the family, "I have an idea!!"Earl remarks, "Of course you do."

◆◆◆

CHAPTER 33

WORD ON THE STREET

The Royal Family is curious about Lizzes' idea. They know that whatever it is, the guardsmen are involved in it. Lizzes asks Valiant, "Would you like a job?" Valiant looks at Lizzes and asks, "Are you serious?" Lizzes replies, "Yes, but it's a hard job." Valiant responds, "I don't care what it is or how hard it is. I will take it." Lizzes replies, "Ok." She instructs the guardsmen to take her to the park. The guardsmen inform the family of the danger just so they are aware. The guardsmen tell them that most of the homeless are alcoholics or drug addicts, "But most of them are just alcoholics, so just be aware." Valiant begins to walk to the park. Lizzes offers, "You can ride with us or with a guardsman."

Valiant replies, "Thank you, but I'm not fit to ride with you. I hope you understand." Lizzes and the Princess begin to get a little emotional. They follow Valiant four blocks to the park. Upon arriving at the park, Lizzes remarks, "It's a lot cleaner than I expected." However, she sees homeless people sleeping on the ground, and she immediately becomes angry. She asks Valiant, "All these people sleep on the ground?!" Valiant confirms, "Yes. But during the wintertime and when it rains, we all sleep under the bridge." Lizzes exclaims, "This isn't right!!" Earl says to Lizzes, "You cannot fix everything!" Lizzes challenges Earl, "Why not!?" Lizzes instructs two guardsmen to go and retrieve 60 guardsmen tents from the palace to set up here for the homeless. She also tells the guardsmen to bring blankets, pillows, and small tent mattresses. Two guardsmen leave for the palace. Lizzes inquires of Valiant, "Are you clean and sober?" Valiant affirms, "Yes! I have to be to help them." Lizzes inquires, "How many of them are clean and sober like you?" Valiant estimates, "Maybe 12 of us."

Lizzes instructs, "Find me the 12, including yourself, and bring them to me." Valiant agrees, "Ok," and begins to gather the 12. He gathers the 12, and the Prince asks Lizzes, "What are you thinking?" The Princess echoes, "Yes, what are you thinking? Your eyes are as big as a bowling ball!!" Lizzes pauses for a moment. Earl asks, "Lizzes, did you hear us?" Lizzes responds, "Yes! You know there is a lot of crime around the country, and criminals like to talk about their crimes to other criminals." She explains, "Who would think twice about talking and telling their plans of criminal mischief around a homeless person sleeping in an alley?" The Prince interjects, “Wait! Are you planning on using homeless people as spies in the cities?”

Lizzes affirms, “Yep! No one would suspect anything from a homeless person. We would know what’s going on in the city before anyone else will.” Earl cautions, “Do you know what will happen if they get caught? They will be killed!!!” Lizzes counters, “Not if they are trained and given weapons to defend themselves if they do come under suspicion.” The Princess remarks, “Well, it is a very good idea if you think about it.” Lizzes suggests, “The guardsmen can train them how to shoot and teach them some defensive techniques.” Earl proposes, “You can also open a homeless shelter in Greater Landing along with a rehab center. They can sleep in the daytime and be out at nighttime. We can also have the 12 alone with Valiant, hang out in the city nightlife, and just listen and gather information.” Lizzes declares, “Excellent, we have a plan.” Just that moment, Valiant shows up with the 12 homeless people.

Lizzes approaches the second person, and it’s a lady, a beautiful lady. Lizzes comments, “You are beautiful. What is your name?” The young woman replies, “Magnolia Wright.” Lizzes inquires, “What is your story?” Magnolia explains, “I traveled here to work at my grandparents’ antique shop. Five months ago, my grandparents got a notice from the bank saying they do not own the shop because of non-payment. Which isn’t true cause they paid the mortgage on the shop every month to these two white men who bought the shop from the bank." Lizzes explains, "Two white men!" Magnolia confirms, "Yes." Lizzes asks, "Did one have a full beard, and the other had a long mustache?" Magnolia asks, "Yes, do you know them?" Lizzes affirms emphatically, "Yes!!!" She adds, "Finish your story." Magnolia continues, "Not only was the mortgage on the shop foreclosed but my grandparents' home was also foreclosed for nonpayment." Lizzes questions, "Do the two white men somehow swindle your grandparents out of their home and business?" Magnolia confirms while crying, "Yes." Lizzes inquires, "Where are your grandparents?" Magnolia reveals, "They both were so hurt that they committed suicide." Lizzes is crying, and so is the Princess.

Magnolia adds, "They had an insurance policy, but it had a no-suicide clause in it. The insurance company offered to cremate them for nothing, and I carry their ashes with me." Lizzes asks, "Did your grandparents have a lawyer to look into their case?" Magnolia responds, "Yes, but they said there was nothing they could do. I think the lawyers were also in on it." Lizzes questions, "Where are you from?" Magnolia answers, "Paris, France. I came here because I am an only child, and I come from an abusive family, which I cannot go back to." Lizzes inquires, "How long have you been on the street?" Magnolia responds, "Five months now. When I left Paris for London, my parents told me not to return and said I was a loser, and they wished I wasn't their child!!" The Princess inquires, "How old are you?" Magnolia answers, "19."

The Princess exclaims, "Oh my God," as she keeps crying. Lizzes instructs Magnolia to give the guardsmen her grandparents' full names, the name of their business, and her identification. She instructs the guardsmen to investigate the involvement of the two white men and the lawyers in the case. Lizzes asks Magnolia, "If you have any of the paperwork from the foreclosure and receipt of payments?" Magnolia confirms, "Yes, I carry that with me, along with pictures of my grandparents." Lizzes directs, "Give all the paperwork to the guardsmen, and we'll take it from here." Magnolia says, "Thank you," wiping tears from her eyes. Lizzes walks up to the third homeless person, an older white man, and inquires, "What is your name and your story?" He responds, "My name is Grayson Wilson, and I am from Manchester. I did ten years in prison and was released three years ago. I was in a major crime family. I got caught stealing, and it was my 3rd offense. I've been on the street for three years now. At the age of 45, with my criminal history, no one is willing to hire me, and I can't blame them. I am not wanted back home. I recently gave my life over to Jesus Christ, my Lord, and Savior, and asked Him to lead me where He wants me to go, and I will follow. He's all I have and all I need. I'm still here, so it must be for a reason."

Lizzes questions, “Do you have any kids?” Grayson responds, “Yes, they are 22 and 24 and hate me because of who I was back then. But I still loved them.” Lizzes inquires, “What about your kids’ mother?” Grayson explains, “I was married to my kids’ mother until they were 13 and 15. I lived a double life for that long until she found out and filed for divorce. With my criminal record, I have no rights to my kids and haven’t seen them since. No visits while I was in jail or any letters. The only reason I know they’re okay is because my mother brought me pictures of them.” Lizzes and the Princess are crying again. Lizzes expresses, “I’m so sorry for your heartache, and I know you must miss your kids.” She requests, “If you don’t mind giving the guardsmen your full name and identification?” She then asks, “Are you clean from drugs and alcohol,” Grayson responds, “Yes, for the last month since I gave my life to Jesus. I have no urge to drink or smoke anymore. It just went away.” Earl exclaims, “Amen!!”Lizzes approaches the fourth homeless person, who is an older white woman.She asks, “What is your name and story?” The lady replies, “My name is Nora Lee. I’m from Canterbury.” Then she explains, “My husband and I moved to London two years ago. He left me for a younger woman and divorced me last year. I went into a deep, deep depression and never got any help for my illness. I’ve never drunk or smoked anything, but I am depressed!” Lizzes questions, “Would you like help with your depression?”

Nora affirms, "Yes! I would love that." Lizzes requests, "Give all of your identification to the guardsmen." Then she walks up to the fifth homeless person and questions, "What is your name and your story?" The fifth man replies, "My name is Roland Wenth." Then he explains, "I'm 32 years old, and I lost my mother to illness. I also went into depression after I had to let go of my job. I'm from London, and I've been homeless for one year." Lizzes inquires, "Are you sober and clean from drugs?" Roland responds, "Yes, I haven't drunk or smoked for the last six months." Lizzes exclaims, "Great, give your identification to the guardsmen." Lizzes walks up to the sixth homeless young lady with a child. Lizzes and Princess screams, "Oh my God! What are you doing in the streets with a child?" The young lady cries, "I've been hiding from an abusive boyfriend." The Princess is in outrage!!

She exclaims, "Hiding on the street with a child! Where are you from?" The young lady explains, "Liverpool. I've been running from city to city, hiding from him. He beat and sexually abused me, and I don't want that to happen to my child. So, I've been on the run. He knows where my parents and friends live in Liverpool and threatened to kill them if they didn't stay out of his business. The police arrest him, but he gets right back out and does it again. So, I just decided to run." Lizzes asserts, "Where does this boyfriend of yours live?" The young lady replies, "He lives in Liverpool, but he's been looking for me and my child." Lizzes directs the guardsmen to take the young lady and her child and put them in her automobile. Lizzes affirms, “As of today, you will run no more.”

She inquires, “Do you have a picture of the young man?” The young lady responds, “Yes,” then hands the picture to Lizzes. Lizzes exclaims, “I’ve seen him!!!” The Princess looks at the picture and remarks, “Yes! He’s at the coffee shop every morning having coffee.” Earl and the Prince examine the picture. Earl observes, “He’s always sitting in a corner by himself, looking at everyone.” The young lady starts to panic and before entering the automobile, she screams, “No, no, I have to get out of here. If he finds me, he will kill me!”Lizzes soothes, “Hey, hey, please calm down! What is your name?” The young lady replies, “Becky Victorium.” Lizzes questions, “How old are you, Becky?” Becky responds, “I’m 24, and I have to get out of here!” Lizzes and the Princess try to calm her down, but she’s in full panic mode; she grabs her child and tries to leave. Lizzes calls out, “Wait, wait!!” Becky stops. Lizzes reassures, “We can protect you! Just trust me.” She insists, “You have to trust me and stop running!!” Then, Becky calms down.

Lizzes instructs two guardsmen to take her and her child and place them in the automobile. She directs a guardsman to begin a search for the young man, and to follow him once found. “I want to know where he’s staying,” She adds, “But first, I want you to blend in. Go to the palace and tell Josephine to dress you in the panther suit. Tell her to give you a 2-hour crash course and demonstration on how to use that suit." The guardsman nods and makes his way to the palace on his horse. The Princess asks Lizzes, "Is that the black suit with claws drawn on the hat, boots, and arm sleeves?" Lizzes confirms, "Yes! It also has a face covering that has claws underneath the eyes." The Princess remarks, "I thought that suit was for a special guardsman." Lizzes responds, "It is, but I feel this is the perfect time to use it." The Princess notes, "The suit looks scary."

Lizzes explains, "Exactly!! It has springs inside the base of the boot that allow the guardsmen to jump 15 feet into the air and has steel claws that come out at the front of the boot and the bottom of the jacket sleeve, which allows the guardsmen to climb buildings and cling to walls. Plus, it has all the weapons the other suits have, and it's almost impossible to see at night."

At that moment, the two guards return with the food. Lizzes instructs the two guardsmen to distribute the food and drinks to the homeless. She informs Valiant, "After they eat, I will continue talking to the other six homeless, but for now, eat and drink as much as you want." Lizzes and the Princess enter the automobile with Becky and her son, while Earl and the Prince help the guardsmen in handing out food to the homeless.

◆◆◆

CHAPTER 34

THE RIGHTEOUS 12

L**izzes** and the Princess are in the automobile having a conversation with Becky. The Princess assures Becky, "You don't have to worry anymore, ok. Lizzes and I want to pray with you. Is that ok?" Becky agrees, "Yes." They all hold hands, including the child. The Princess begins to pray, "Lord, you said if two came into agreement in your name, it shall come to pass. Well, we have four coming into agreement right now. We thank you in advance for covering Becky and her child and keeping them out of danger. We pray that you put a shield of armor around her and her child to protect them from danger that they cannot see. We pray that you will touch her family back home and give them a new mind and a new way of thinking. Now, Lord, we want to thank you for the blessing you have and will continue to store on her life. Now, Lord, watch over us as we continue to go through this journey. We say this prayer in the name of the Father, the Son, and the Holy Spirit. Amen."

After lunch, Lizzes and Earl exit the automobile. Valiant is now bringing the other six homeless individuals over to talk to Lizzes. Lizzes walks up to the seventh person and asks, "What is your name and your story?" It's a young black man. He introduces himself, "My name is Ellison Rogers. I am from Bordeaux, France. I was a thief. I served five years in prison and needed a new start in a new city. I wash dishes in the African food restaurant in Greater Landing, but I can't afford to pay rent right now so I sleep on the street until I can do better." Lizzes inquires, "Are you sober and clean from drugs?" The young man Ellison affirms, "Yes!" Lizzes responds, "Great, give all of your identification to the guardsmen." Lizzes approaches the eighth person. Valiant mentions, "I know these next four personally. This is Michael Johnson, 32, from Canterbury. He was an alcoholic but has been sober for three months now. This Gable Ramon, 37, from Canterbury, was an alcoholic who had been sober for five months." He explains to Lizzes about the men, one by one, while pointing at them.

He then points at the man and explains, "This is Wyndham Hill, 30, from Liverpool. He was an alcoholic, been sober for seven months." Then goes to another one, "This is Landon Johnson, 41, an alcoholic, been sober for eight months from London." Then Valiant clarifies, "These four were in a gang together, stole and robbed people. They all went to prison together for six hard years. They are now devoted Christians and preach the word of God on the streets to whoever will listen. But no one gives them a job with their backgrounds. So, they do what they can and help protect the others." Lizzes is amazed at the men's transformation. She comforts them, "All of your prayers have just been answered." The four men begin to thank God. Lizzes directs them to give all of their identification to the guardsmen. Lizzes then inquires of the lead guardsman, "In that abandoned apartment building in Greater Landing, how long will it take you to get it up and operating?"

The guardsman reports, "We have gone through that building, and everything looks good, just need to have electrical power and water and some touches here and there, maybe a month." Lizzes responds, "Good, let's get that project started." Lizzes tells the 12, "We have an apartment building that will be opening at the end of the month. I'm going to put you in it. Then there is another building that we have that's completely empty, but it has power. It needs to be clean, but it will hold all of the homeless, and we can also have a rehabilitation center inside that building for the homeless who want to go there. But, for the homeless to stay in that building, they will have to sign up for the rehabilitation process."

Lizzes then declares, "I will have a couple of my guardsmen start the cleaning process tomorrow and you can move whoever homeless wants to go tomorrow night." Valiant exclaims, "Thank you! You won't regret it." Just then, the two guardsmen who went to fetch the tents, pillows, and mattresses show up with seven more guards and two carriages full of equipment. Lizzes informs the 12, "You will now be known as 'The Righteous 12.' Your main job will be to help and protect the homeless, the churches, and the bullied by all means necessary. You will go through 8 hours of training for six weeks, and you will get uniforms with the guardsmen patch—a patch that says 'The Righteous 12.' You will be under the protection of the guardsmen, so you will be appointed a head guardsman to whom you will report." Lizzes invites Becky to come and stand in line. She asks everyone, "If this is something that they want to do?" They all respond affirmatively, "Yes!" Lizzes acknowledges, "Ok." She instructs the guardsmen to come and have them repeat the guardsmen's oath and sign their letter of protection. Once the tents are set up, Lizzes instructs two guardsmen to watch over them until 7 pm. She instructs Valiant to prepare the homeless for the shelter tomorrow night. Lizzes announces, "You 12 will begin your training next week." Lizzes directs Becky to ride with her and informs her, "I have a special place for you."

Lizzes and the rest of the Royal Family leave the park. She instructs her driver to stop at her home. Lizzes, Earl, Becky, the Prince, and her child enter the house. Lizzes informs, "Becky, this is your new home." Becky looks at Lizzes, then she looks at everyone else and exclaims, "Is this for real?" Lizzes affirms, "Yes!!

This is your new home. No more sleeping on the street with that child!!" Becky is in disbelief. She expresses, "I don't know what to do. Where do I start?" Lizzes suggests, "You can start by relaxing. You have nothing to worry about. You will go into training next week. Your child will stay with my coworkers and go to school with them. What is your child's name?" Becky shares, "His name is Brice, and he's six years old." Lizzes assures, "You and Brice will be protected and escorted by the guardsmen until you are trained and can protect yourself. Don't worry about your ex-boyfriend looking for you. We will find him and let him know that you and your son are protected by the guardsmen. Believe me, being confronted by a guardsman is the scariest situation ever. And he will be confronted by seven guardsmen, and that is unbelievably scary."

Becky alarmingly says, "I know my ex; he will not go easy." Lizzes states, "He will go easy or go hard. That will be his choice." Lizzes tries to turn the conversation and suggests, "Let me show you the house." While showing her the house, she explains, "This room is an escape room." She shows her the trap door and informs, "If you ever need to escape, come into this room, hit this panel five times like this, and the panel will open."

Lizzes leads Becky downstairs and notifies, "Make sure you lock the door behind you. Here, these are my personal writings; do not read them. The butler from the palace will be coming here two times a week and he will put my writings right here. So, if you see him, don't be alarmed. Just let him in." Becky agrees, "Ok." They then head back upstairs. She clarifies, "Remember, after you reenter from downstairs, knock on the door five times to lock it." She then shows Becky the bathroom, "For now, wash up, and we will pick you up to have coffee with us in the morning. There is food here. You can cook breakfast. We will see you in the morning." Becky expresses gratitude, "Thank you. I don't know how I can ever pay you back." Lizzes soothes her, "You don't have to pay me back. Just take care of yourself and your son." Becky assures, "I promise you, I will."

As the Royal Family leaves the house, the guardsman in charge of searching for Becky's ex arrives. He informs Lizzes that he found the young lady's ex. Lizzes immediately questions, "Where?" The guardsman replies, "He's at the Local Bar." Lizzes asks, "What's the name of the bar?" The guardsman confirms, "That's it! The Local Bar." Lizzes directs, "Ok, take seven guardsmen and go to the bar, and I want to make sure he knows not to bother Becky ever again." The lead guardsman takes six guardsmen from the Royal Family's escort, which consists of 12, and heads towards the bar. Earl expresses concern, "I pray to God that the young man doesn't start any trouble with the guardsmen." Lizzes agrees, "Me also," looking nervously towards Earl.

The family arrives back at the palace. As they exit their automobiles, the Prince and the Princess walk up to Earl and Lizzes with a look of concern. Lizzes asks the Princess, “What’s wrong?” The Princess admits, “We are nervous!” Lizzes inquires, “Why?” The Princess explains, “You heard what Becky said about her ex. She said he’s very confrontational, arrogant, and has no respect for authority. That combination is a death sentence if acted towards a guardsman. We most definitely don’t want the guardsmen to kill anyone, but they’re trained to defuse any threat by all means necessary when threatened.” Lizzes acknowledges, “Yeah, we have been feeling the same way.” She suggests, “I think we should go to that bar before anything happens.” The Prince objects, “No! We should not interfere with any guardsmen’s orders. Once the order is given, no matter which one of us gives it, only the King and Queen have the authority to stop it. We should leave it alone and let Becky’s ex dictate his fate.” They all walk into the palace, visibly nervous!!

◆◆◆

CHAPTER 35

THE LOCAL BAR FIGHT

As the Royal Family sits nervously at home, the seven guardsmen arrive at The Local Bar's back entrance. They dismount their horses—three enter through the back and four through the front, all in Royal attire. Everyone inside stops what they're doing. They have never seen a Royal Guardsman in any bar, and certainly not seven of them. The locals realize the guardsmen are either looking for someone or that something terrible is about to happen. While the four guardsmen stand on patrol, the other three scope the room. While they scope the room, they find their target. Becky's ex is seated with three other gentlemen, all of whom are armed. The guardsmen see everything, and all seven make eye contact, quickly forming a plan with just that eye contact.

The lead guardsman walks towards Becky's ex and asks, "Sir, may I please talk to you outside?" The gentleman replies, "What's this about?" The lead guardsman tells, "It's about Becky!" The young man jumps up and exclaims, "Becky!! How do you know Becky?" The guardsman mentions, "Sir, I'm going to need you to calm down and don't make any threatening movements!" The young man shouts, "Shut up!! Don't tell me what to do! I ask you a question! Where is Becky?" Realizing the gentleman is beyond reasoning, the guardsman issues another warning, "Sir, I will not ask you again. Please calm down and step outside, and I will tell you about Becky." The gentleman is now in an uncontrollable rage. The gentleman picks up a glass of beer, throws it against the wall, and screams, "Where's Becky??" The three other men also stand up. They inform the guardsmen, "We have been paid by this gentleman to find Becky and his son. Now, we don't want any trouble with the guardsmen, but we have been paid a lot of money, and we are not giving it back. So, if you don't mind, please tell us where she is, and we will do our job that we have been paid to do, and there won't be any problems."

Six gentlemen at the bar also stand. The lead guardsman looks at the gentlemen at the bar. He then turns, glances at the guardsmen, and gives a nod. The guardsman states, "Becky is now under the protection of the guardsmen. Any more threats or pursuit of her will not end well for you. I'm asking you to leave her alone or suffer the consequences." The guardsman then questions the gentleman, "What is your decision?" Becky's ex declares, "I don't care who you are or what protection she has. I will find her, and when I do, I guarantee she won't ever leave again," as he takes a step closer to the guardsman. The guardsman clarifies, "You have been warned," and turns to leave. The gentleman grabs a beer glass full of beer and throws it at the lead guardsman, all the while screaming, "Where is Becky!!" The guardsman hears the glass coming towards him, swiftly turns around, dodges it, and then catches the beer glass. Then, flings it back at the gentleman.

The glass hits the gentleman on the forehead, knocking him out. The six men at the bar reach for the guns. The guardsmen hit all six men on both hands with their whips. Their whips lashed so hard and fast that they split open the backs of all six gentlemen's hands. Both of the men's hands are bleeding and cut up, so they are not able to use them. The six gentlemen are looking at their hands and screaming in pain. They are all hit in the foreheads with the handle part of the guardsmen's whips and are knocked completely out, causing them to fall to the floor. The lead guardsman is now staring directly at the other three men who are paid to find Becky! The lead guardsman declares to them, "You can suffer the consequences, or you and your men leave and don't ever return." The men raise their hands and exclaim, "We are leaving!!!" They grab Becky's ex, who is just now waking up. Becky's ex inquires, "What happened?" One of the three men explains, "You got knocked out by the guardsmen."

The gentleman is bleeding from his forehead, and the other six gentlemen are bleeding from both hands. Just then, a doctor and two nurses show up. The guardsmen had already informed them of what was going to happen at the Local Bar and told them to get there as fast as they could. The doctor and nurses begin bandaging the men's wounds who are just waking up. The doctor advises the guardsmen, "These men aren't well enough to travel. You should give them three days to heal up a little." Becky's ex vows, "As soon as I'm healed, I will be back!" The guardsman informs the men and Becky's ex, "After three days, you will leave, but you! you shall be taken to the town jail for attacking and trying to do bodily harm to a guardsman."

The guardsman then declares, "I was going to let you go if you choose not to come back, but I can see the only thing that's going to stop you from finding Becky is Death or jail, and us guardsmen aren't in the killing mood today."

After the nurses finish bandaging the men, three guardsmen instruct the six to follow the doctor and nurses to the doctor's office, where they will stay for three days. The guardsman warns the three men, "You can go as you please, but I warned you not to look for Becky cause if you do, you will witness a terrible fate." The guardsmen are so focused on the men that they forget the bar is full of people, and they all look terrified!! After Becky's ex gets bandage, he jumps out of the chair and attacks the guardsman by swinging a punch at him.

The guardsman ducks under the punch, uses the man's body weight, moves forward to pick him up by the waist, walks towards the window, and throws him out of it. The two Nurses run outside to check to see if he's alive. The gentleman is breathing but is knocked out cold again. The doctor instructs the three men to pick him up and bring him to the doctor's office. The doctor advises the guardsman, "I don't think this man needs to go to jail. I think he needs psychiatric help!!!" The guardsman concedes, "You may be right, but for now, he will be handcuffed to his bed so he doesn't endanger anyone else." As the men are escorted to the doctor's office, the lead guardsman directs the other guardsmen, "Make sure the gentleman is handcuffed," they also handcuff his legs. He informs the three men, "You are free to go after you leave the doctor's office, but I'm leaving a guardsman to watch you just in case you get any ideas of trying to find Becky."

The lead guardsman goes back inside the bar and apologizes to the patrons. He also informs the bartender to add any damages to the Royal Family's account. The people in the bar are just staring at the guardsman in complete shock at what they just witnessed. The guardsman then turns and exits the bar. When they reach the doctor's office, the nursing staff helps the men get settled in their rooms. The doctors examine their wounds and realize they all need about 60 stitches on each hand. The doctors are amazed at the accuracy of the guardsman's strikes. The lead guardsman arrives at the doctor's office. He enters, and the doctors update him on the damage done to the six men and Becky's ex. The doctors inform the guardsman, "There is a psychiatric hospital on two days travel. This man is not stable at all!! I suggest that after these three days, he be admitted there. I will get you all the information and make the arrangements myself." The lead guardsman accepts and says, "Go ahead and make the arrangements." The doctor confirms, "Should we add the fees to the Queen's account or the Royal Family account?" The lead guardsman orders, "Add the fees to the Royal Family's account and split the fees up between the two, the Prince and Princess and the Duchess and the Duke." The doctor acknowledges, "Ok." The guardsman states, "I want to see the gentleman that attacked me." The nurse takes him to the gentleman. The gentleman is handcuffed by his hands and feet. He is semi-conscious and being watched by a guardsman.

The gentleman sees the lead guardsman, and he immediately tries to get out of the handcuffs, but he can't. He begins yelling at the lead guardsman, demanding, "Where is Becky?" The lead guardsman reaches for his whip. Seeing this, the man calms down immediately. The lead guardsman remarks, "Yeah, you're not as crazy as the doctors are making you out to be." Then he informs the man, "Did you know Becky was living on the street with your son? Just because she was running from you!" He adds, "Yeah, she was living with the homeless!" The gentleman now has this calm and sad look on his face.

The guardsman recounts, "She told us she was running from city to city, living on the street with the homeless all because of you. We, the guardsmen, are peacekeepers of the people, and once someone is under the protection of the guardsmen's peacekeepers agreement, they cannot be harmed or touched by anyone. If they are harmed or touched, the consequences are life imprisonment or death! We see the bruises on Becky that were given to her by you." Then the guardsman informs the man, "The doctors want to put you in a psychiatric hospital for a long time." The gentleman responds calmly, "I'm not crazy!"

The lead guardsman declares, "Well, I'm going to give you a choice. You will never see Becky or your son ever again unless you change. Now, here is your choice. You can go to prison for three years for attacking a guardsman, and that's being generous cause it is 15 to 20 years in prison for attacking a guardsman. I'll give you three days to make your decision." The guardsman then leaves the room, finds one of the doctors, and instructs him, "Don't make the appointment to the psychiatric hospital. I had a talk with the gentleman, and he will give his decision in three days." As the lead guardsman and his team leave the doctor's office, they see the ten guardsmen and the three Chinese men heading their way.

◆◆◆

CHAPTER 36

THE VENOMOUS TWENTY

As ten guardsmen approach with the three Chinese men. The two guardsmen that Lizzes assigns to help move the homeless to the new shelter arrive at the Local Bar. They notice the glass is scattered across the sidewalk and ask the manager, "What happened?" The manager explains, "There had been a bar fight that ended with seven people needing stitches at the doctor's office." One of the guardsmen asks, "Was anyone seriously injured?" The manager replies, "Yes." the guardsman says, "Alright, that's all we need to know," and the two head toward the palace.

Meanwhile, the ten guardsmen escorting the Chinese men arrive at the doctor's office. They all head towards the palace to meet Lizzes. After arriving at the palace, the guardsmen take the 3 Chinese men into Lizzes and Earl's study. The guardsman on duty informs Lizzes, "Three Chinese men have arrived, and they are in your study." Lizzes is very excited. She grabs Earl and instructs the guardsmen on duty, "Find the Prince and Princess and bring them to my study." Lizzes runs to the study. As she enters, the three Chinese men get up and bow to show their respect and tradition. While Lizzes and Earl shake their hands and introduce themselves, the Prince and Princess come in. Lizzes introduces the Prince and Princess. The three Chinese men show their respect by bowing to them. The Prince and Princess shake their hands. Then, they all take a seat. Lizzes asks the Chinese men their names. All three are fit and in top physical condition as they introduce themselves as Chan Lee, Won Chon, and Wang Fu.

Lizzes observes, "I see you speak perfect English. What other languages do you speak?" Wang Fu replies, "We speak Chinese and French." Lizzes says, "That's perfect. I'm sure you're wondering why I asked the guardsmen to bring you here." Wang Fu nods, "Yes, we are." Lizzes questions, "My husband and I were on that ship two years ago when we saw you practicing. What type of martial arts were you practicing?" Wang Fu responds, "Kung fu." Lizzes says, "I was hoping you could train our guardsmen in martial arts," Wang Fu asks, "For how long?" Lizzes responds, "For as long as it takes to become experts or masters," Wang Fu shakes his head and explains, "To become an expert, a master takes decades. But to become good enough to protect yourself, with lots of training, will take one year." Lizzes inquires, "How many styles of kung fu do you practice?" Wang Fu answers, "We are masters in 14 styles."

The Royal Family exchanges excited glances. Lizzes requests, "I'd like to show you something." The Chinese men get up, bow, and follow the family to a work area where four guardsmen are ready to demonstrate the super suits. After the demonstration, the Chinese men are eager to combine their kung fu skills with the super suits. Lizzes asks, "So, will you train our guardsmen?" Wang Fu replies, "We would be honored. But we will need somewhere that's private and very difficult to get to in order to have complete focus." Lizzes nods, "We have several buildings you can use in Greater Landing." The Chinese men agree on the location. Lizzes shares, "I think I have the perfect building. It has four floors and can accommodate 35 to 40 guardsmen on each floor. It also has a private backyard that sits on five acres of land, separated from other buildings."

Wang Fu requests, "Can you take us to the building tomorrow?" Lizzes agrees, "Yes." Then, she instructs the ten guardsmen to accompany the Chinese men to the building and stay with them until construction is complete. She adds, "Charge everything to the Royal Family's account, not the King's or Queen's." Before they leave, Lizzes questions, "How long will it take to convert the building into your training facility?" Wang Fu replies, "No more than three days if the building is in good condition." Lizzes says, "Okay. I have 20 guardsmen who need to be in France in three months. With eight hours of training every day, what level would they reach?" Wang Fu explains, "There are ten stages in each of the 14 styles of kung fu. With eight hours of training a day, they should reach the first stage of one style in three months. We will let you know when training will begin. Your guardsmen already have some martial training, so it shouldn't take long for them to learn. But for now, we are very tired and wish to rest."

Lizzes directs the guardsmen to take the Chinese men to the Hotel London, place them on the Royal floor, and have four guardsmen stand guard. She instructs the other six guardsmen to take the Chinese men's belongings to the building in Greater Landing. After the Chinese men depart from the palace, the Queen enters Lizzes' study. The Queen shares, "You know, the guardsmen are already superb fighters. With this training and those suits, they will be the most feared force in the world."

Lizzes is stunned and asks, "How do you know all this? You weren't in the meeting or at the demonstration." The Queen smiles and explains, "My child, for someone so smart, you haven't learned anything from living in this house." She exits the room, leaving Lizzes in confusion. As Lizzes is feeding Princess Lizzie, the guard on duty enters and informs her about the local bar fight. Lizzes questions, "Are the men okay?" The guardsman replies, "Yes. They're resting at the doctor's office for the next few days. Then they'll leave London. But Becky's ex will be going to jail or a psychiatric hospital." Lizzes happily responds, "Good. I'll inform Becky tomorrow."

Meanwhile, at the Hotel London, the guardsmen escort the Chinese men inside. As they approach the front desk, they notice two white men with an entourage of six others staring at them. The Chinese men also sense the tension. The guardsmen immediately stop and begin to stare angrily at the men. The two white men and their entourage turn from looking at the guardsmen as they keep walking. As the men exit the hotel, two guardsmen walk outside behind them, stop, and begin to stare at them as they walk across the street. The men do not dare to anger the guardsmen as that will be seen as a threat, and the guardsmen will act accordingly.

Wang, the oldest of the Chinese men, explains, "Those men will be trouble for you. We don't know the situation between your guardsmen and those men, but a storm is brewing. Prepare yourselves for a fight." The three Chinese men check in to the hotel and are then escorted to their rooms. The guardsmen searched the rooms before allowing the Chinese men in and also set up posts at each of their doors. Meanwhile, across the street, at a corner bar, the two white men and their entourage are curious about the Chinese men. They approach the bartender, Sid. One of the white men introduces himself, "Hi, do you know who we are?" The bartender responds, "Yes, you're Jack and John Dweet. Everyone knows who you are."

Jack hands Sid a thick wad of money and inquires, “Who in this bar would you least want to meet in an alley?” Sid looks around and says, “Edward Williamson.” Jack nods and asks, “We know him. He’s a former boxer and guardsman. Didn’t he go to prison for beating up four guardsmen at once because he refused an assignment and refused to be disciplined?” Sid replies, “Yes. He spent five years in prison. It took six guardsmen to bring him down.” John hands Sid more money and questions, “Where can we find Mr. Edward Williamson?” Sid points, “Look behind you. He’s the 6’8, 275-pound white guy sitting by himself in the corner.”

The two brothers share gratitude to Sid and approach Mr. Williamson’s table. “Mr. Edward Williamson?” Jack asks. “Who wants to know?” Edward responds by looking up at the two brothers. The brothers try to introduce themselves, but Mr. Williamson cuts them off and says, “No need for introductions. I know who you are. What do you want? You’re interrupting my alone time.” Jack lays down a thick wad of money and clarifies, “Mr. Williamson, we’d like to buy your services.” Edward looks at the money on the table, grabs it, and says, “Follow me out back.” The three men walk out the back door into the alley. They look around to make sure they are alone, noticing only two homeless men with their carts waiting for food from the kitchen staff. Ignoring the homeless men, they begin to discuss business.

CHAPTER 37

THE PRINCESS BALL

It's the night of the Princess Ball. People from all over the country arrive in town and are preparing themselves for the event. Meanwhile, back at the palace, Lizzes and her coworkers are excited because they get to reveal the new Royal Guardsmen's event uniforms, the Royal Family's event uniforms, and the new casual pants and dress suits for the Royal Guardsmen. Lizzes informs her coworkers, "I'm going to get the head guardsman. I want to fit him with his new uniform first. Then, we'll get the rest of the guardsmen fitted."

Lizzes goes to fetch the head guardsman while the other ladies get the uniforms ready. When Lizzes returns with him and requests, "If you don't mind, please step into the dressing room and try on this uniform." She hands him the new uniform, and he responds with one word: "Magnificent!" He steps into the dressing room, and the ladies smile, knowing he loves the uniform. When he steps out, Lizzes and her coworkers are amazed at how well it fits.

The uniform pants are gold with two pearl-white stripes running down the outside of each leg. The jacket is pearl-white with a collar laced in gold stripes. The buttons are gold, and the shoulders have two to four blue stripes laced with gold. The ends of the jacket sleeves are trimmed in gold, and the sleeves feature four buttons each. The shirt is dark blue silk with gold buttons, and there are two gold and blue ropes over and under both shoulders. The hat is a shorter version of the Royal Guardsmen's hats but in blue, matching with the shoes and belt, that has a gold buckle. The gloves are white on the outside and gold on the inside. The guardsman looks in the mirror; the suit fits perfectly, and he loves it.

Lizzes asks the head guardsman to wait in the waiting room while they fit the other guardsmen. The rest of the guardsmen's uniforms are the exact opposite of the head guardsman's, with white pants, gold stripes, and a gold jacket. After fitting the guardsmen, Lizzes leaves to fetch the King and Queen. As Lizzes is walking back to the dressing room with the King and Queen, the head guardsman walks out of the waiting room, heading toward the kitchen. The Queen sees and stops him. She walks up to the head palace guardsman and begins to check out his uniform. Lizzes is nervous because she really wants her approval. As the Queen is checking out the palace guardsman uniform, the King leans over to

Lizzes and compliments, "You've outdone yourself. That uniform is spectacular!" The Queen finishes her inspection and turns to Lizzes, exclaiming, "This uniform is extravagant! Your brain is something to marvel at." Lizzes is overwhelmed with joy and excitement as she responds, "Thank you, Your Majesty!"

Lizzes then informs, "Now, if you would follow me to the dressing room, we can get you fitted and dressed." The Queen and King enter the dressing room with Lizzes, and her coworkers bow, saying, "Your Majesty, you are first." Lizzes presents the Queen with her dress for the ball, pulling it out of the closet for her to see. The Queen is overwhelmed with joy, tears welling up in her eyes. The dress is slim-cut to fit the Queen's figure, made of silk blue with gold lace trim around the bottom. It's V-cut around the neck with lace gold trim, and the hem is slightly lifted in the middle so that only the sparkling blue diamond shoes are visible when she walks. The dress has short sleeves paired with long silk blue gloves that extend to the forearm. The ensemble is completed with diamond blue raindrop earrings outlined in gold and a matching blue diamond pearl necklace. The Queen's crown is gold-plated with ten blue diamond stones around the top and thirty small blue diamond stones around the bottom. The Queen, with joy, tells Lizzes, "You've outdone yourself. This dress is amazing! I can't wait to see what the King's uniform looks like."

At that moment, a guardsman enters and informs, “Excuse me, Duchess, but we have received word from WOTS that the Dweet brothers and their associates are planning an attack on Greater Landing tonight during the Princess Ball. How would you like to handle this?” Lizzes explains, “Send twelve guardsmen to locate the men and have them followed. Put the security guards in Greater Landing on high alert. Once the brothers and their entourage enter Greater Landing, have the guardsmen show their presence. That should make them think twice about following through with their plans.” The guardsman replies, “At once,” and leaves the room. The Queen inquires of Lizzes, “Is everything okay?” Lizzes reassures her, “Yes, Your Majesty.” Then, she turns to her coworkers, saying, “Let’s finish fitting the King and then the Prince and Princess.”

Lizzes presents the King with his uniform. The King opens the suit bag and pulls out his uniform, marveling at its magnificence. The jacket is dark blue silk with a gold collar that extends from the neck down both sides of the jacket. It features four gold and four blue ropes that drape over each shoulder and attach to the jacket’s middle outside. A golden silk piece runs over the ropes on both shoulders, fastening with blue buttons at the end. The jacket collar extends up to the top of the neck, buttoning at the top with gold buttons running down to the bottom of the jacket. The pants are also blue silk, paired with black diamond shoes with leather soles. The King’s crown is blue and gold, adorned with twelve gold diamonds around the top and twenty-four small gold diamonds around the bottom. The King, overwhelmed with excitement, can't wait to show it off.

Lizzes takes the Queen and King to the picture room, where the photographer and staff are amazed by what they see. The photographer says to Lizzes, "Your mind is something I've never seen before. It's like you've seen the future or something. These designs are definitely futuristic." Lizzes modestly replies, "Thank you," and instructs the photographer to take as many shots as needed. She asks the Queen and King to remain in the room after the photo session to keep the Royal Family hidden until the proper moment.

Lizzes then returns to the dressing room and asks the guardsmen to bring in the Princess and Prince. "Are you ready?" Lizzes asks the Princess, who excitedly replies, "Yes! Hurry up! I can't stand the excitement." Lizzes opens the dress bag and reveals the Princess's dress: a silk maroon gown with a V-cut neckline and short sleeves. The necklace is white gold with twenty maroon diamonds that shine around her neck. She has two bracelets for each wrist, made of small white diamonds and gold-plated. The shoes are maroon diamonds, and the dress is slim-cut to fit the Princess's figure perfectly. Lizzes asks the Princess to step out of the dressing room. Everyone is stunned, and her coworkers tell the Princess, "You look absolutely beautiful!" The Princess, overwhelmed, admires herself in the mirror. Lizzes then says, “Hold on, here’s the final touch.” She unveils a diamond-plated Princess crown with twelve maroon diamonds on top and twenty-four maroon sparkling diamonds around the bottom. The Princess looks at herself in the mirror and says to Lizzes and her coworkers, “You ladies are absolutely amazing!” The ladies blush and say, “Thank you!”

Next, it’s the Prince’s turn. Lizzes opens the suit bag and pulls out the Prince’s uniform. The jacket is similar to the King’s but in maroon, with only two ropes over and under each shoulder instead of four. The buttons are gold, fastening up to the neck, where the jacket is laced with two gold feathers on both sides. The sleeves end with two gold stripes, and there are four gold buttons on each shoulder. The pants are silk black with maroon stripes running down the outside, and the shoes are black leather. Lizzes then directs, “Now, let’s put on the Prince’s crown.” She unveils the crown, which is maroon with twelve white diamonds on the top and twenty-four white diamonds around the bottom.

The Princess tells the Prince, “You look amazing and handsome.” The Prince blushes as he admires himself in the mirror. Lizzes then asks the Princess and Prince to follow her into the photography room. As they enter, they see the King and Queen, and they all stare at each other in admiration. Lizzes, smiling from a corner, instructs the photographer to take several pictures. She then leaves the room to change into her dress, which is identical to the

Princess's but in grass green. The Duchess's crown is white diamond-plated with green diamonds, while the Duke's uniform matches the Prince's but with a silk green jacket and black pants with green stripes down both legs. The Duke's crown is also similar to the Prince's, with green diamonds.

Lizzes directs her three coworkers to go and get dressed and meet them in the waiting room with the palace guardsmen. Lizzes' three coworkers have uniforms just like the palace guardsmen, except theirs are dresses. Lizzes and Earl enter the photography room, where the family is smiling and congratulating Lizzes. They all take a family picture.

Lizzes takes a peek out of the photography room, located upstairs above the ballroom, and sees guests starting to arrive. She instructs the head palace guardsman to get everyone in their rightful places so the Royal Family can be introduced. The head palace guardsman goes to position all the palace guardsmen around the ballroom. He then begins to introduce himself and welcome the guests to the palace. The butler, kitchen staff, and servers look flamboyant in their black-and-white attire, also designed by Lizzes and her coworkers. There are guests from countries like France, Belgium, Ireland, the Netherlands, Denmark, and the entire British Royal Family. Some of the richest families in England are also present.

The ballroom is now nearly filled with guests. A guardsman comes up the stairs to inform the Princess that everyone is here and to see if the Royal Family is ready for their introduction. The Queen notices that Lizzes and Earl are really nervous, pacing up and down the room since they've never attended a formal ball with such important people present. She walks up to both of them and instructs, "Stop pacing up and down! Stand up straight," as she straightens out their attire. "This is not the time to show signs of nervousness! Not after all you have done and accomplished so far. Now, take a deep breath because you're being introduced first."

Lizzes and Earl calm down. The Queen informs the head palace guardsman, "We are ready." The guardsman says, "Okay," and escorts Lizzes, Earl, the King, and the Queen down the back stairs to the side entrance of the ballroom. The Prince and the Princess will be walking down the main staircase into the ballroom for their introduction. The Queen, King, Lizzes, and Earl are now behind the curtain on the ballroom floor. The head palace guardsman says to the crowd, "Ladies and gentlemen, may I have your attention, please? I now introduce to you the new Duke and Duchess of Sussex." Lizzes and Earl acquired that title from the Queen when the Queen and King's youngest son died from pneumonia at the age of 19 and adopted Lizzes and Earl. He had no wife or children. Lizzes and Earl step from behind the curtain, and there is a pin-drop silence in the ballroom. The crowd is so amazed by their attire that they forget to clap. Then, all of a sudden, a scream of excitement erupts from the crowd as they marvel at Lizzes and Earl. "Magnificent, beautiful, and elegant" are the words that are used by the crowd as Lizzes and Earl are escorted to their seats.

The head guardsman walks back to the curtain as Lizzes whispers to Earl, "I'm glad that's over; I almost passed out!" Earl replies, "You and I both." The head palace guardsman then says, "Ladies and gentlemen, I now introduce to you the king and Queen." The king and Queen step from behind the curtain, and the crowd goes ballistic! They are amazed by the King and Queen's attire, and the crowd lets them know as they gossip and admire their outfits. The Queen whispers to the King, "Lizzes has outdone herself again!" The King responds, "I know. Just wait till the Prince and Princess come walking down the stairs." The Queen and King take their places at the royal table beside Lizzes and Earl.

Then, the head guardsman walks to the end of the stairs. He says, "Ladies and gentlemen, I now introduce to you the Prince and Princess of Wales." The Prince and Princess enter the stairway. They begin to wave, and the crowd erupts at the sight of them in their outfits. The people in the crowd are saying, "Look how beautiful they look! Look at their outfits; they look amazing. I wonder who made their clothes. I want that dress," the women are saying.

As the Prince and Princess make their way downstairs, one of the six palace guardsmen standing on the stairs notices someone in the crowd. As the Prince and Princess take their places at the royal table, the palace guardsman walks up to Lizzes. Leaning down, he asks her, "Duchess, isn't that Jack and John Dweet to your left?" Lizzes looks and makes contact with the brothers. Both brothers raise their champagne glasses as they acknowledge Lizzes noticing them. She asks, "Any word on the 12 guardsmen that were sent to find and follow the brothers?" The palace guardsman replies, "Not yet, but I'll find out. For now, what would you like me to do about the brothers?" Lizzes says, "Nothing, just keep your eye on them. Something isn't right."

CHAPTER 38

CONFRONTATION AT THE GATE

M**eanwhile**, the 12 guardsmen reach the south and north entry gates into Greater Landing. They see no one! They can't find any of the Dweet brothers' entourage or the Dweet brothers themselves. The guardsman inquires of the security guards, "Have you seen anyone trying to enter Greater Landing without identifying themselves?" The security guards respond, "No! Should we be on guard?" The guardsman instructs, "Yes! Put all your security guards on alert and check the city for any unusual activity." The guardsmen sense that something isn't right.

At that moment, one of the guardsmen comes riding from the palace on horseback. He says to the lead guardsman, "The Dweet brothers are at the Princess Ball. The Duchess asked me to find you and find out what's going on in Greater Landing." The lead guardsman is now very curious. He tells the other guardsmen, "We haven't found anything wrong or any sign of the Dweet brothers' entourage." The lead guardsman muses, "Huh, the brothers are at the ball!" He then instructs the guardsmen to head back to the palace and inform the Duchess. He orders the remaining 11 guardsmen to spread out and check Greater Landing with the security guards.

As the 11 guardsmen and 22 security guards are inspecting Greater Landing for anything suspicious, the lead guardsman and two security guards see a figure walking toward them. As the figure gets closer, it gets bigger. Once the figure is in plain sight, the lead guardsman recognizes who it is—it's Mr. Williamson! The two security guards immediately stand at attention, hands on their weapons. The lead guardsman tells them to stand down. The security guards notice how tall and imposing Mr. Williamson is. The lead guardsman is no slouch himself, but even though Mr. Williamson stands 6'8" and weighs 275 lbs, the lead guardsman, at 6'5" and about 250 lbs, is still slightly smaller. The lead guardsman and Mr. Williamson begin to walk until they are within three feet of each other.

The lead guardsman says, "Mr. Williamson, it's been a long time." Mr. Williamson responds, "Yes, it has, Guardsman." Although Mr. Williamson knows the guardsman by name, he also knows it's disrespectful to address a guardsman by name since he was once one himself. The lead guardsman questions, "We heard that there was going to be trouble in Greater Landing by an entourage that the Dweet brothers put together. Do you know anything about that?" Mr. Williamson replies, "Sure, but how do you know about that?" The lead guardsman informs, "We have our sources." Mr. Williamson says, "Okay, I see. You have spies around the city." The lead guardsman responds, "Once a guardsman, always a guardsman."

Mr. Williamson continues, "Yeah, I was approached by the brothers, and they offered me a lot of money for my services and the trouble they wanted to start in Greater Landing, but I turned them down. I told them that it would be stupid for you two brothers and six men to go and start trouble with the guardsmen. I told them they would hunt you down until they found you. You wouldn't be safe anywhere, and you don't stand a chance in a fight with them. So, the brothers changed their minds about their plans. But those brothers are out to destroy the guardsmen and everything they stand for, so you may want to keep a close eye on them."

The lead guardsman clarifies, "We have eyes on the brothers, but I'm curious why you turned them down." Mr. Williamson responds, "Well, as you already know, my parents are the Prince and Princess of Kent. So, you know who I am and what I am. I've disrespected my family enough, and it's time to right a wrong. Just because of who I am doesn't mean I'm perfect. I've made some terrible mistakes, but now that I'm older and have been through what I've been through, I've learned a lot of patience. Have a good day, guardsman."

Mr. Williamson begins to walk away. The lead guardsman mutters softly to himself, “The young man has finally grown up.” The guardsman then calls out, “Hey, Mr. Williamson!” As Mr. Williamson is walking away, he says, “You should stop by the palace and say hi to the family. I’m sure they would love to see you, especially the Prince.” Mr. Williamson stops, turns around, and says, “I will, when the time is right,” and disappears into the night.

One of the security guards questions, “Who was that man?” The guardsman responds, “A Prince and a former guardsman who went down the wrong path but seems to have found his way back.” The security guard inquires, “If he’s a Prince, where are his Royal Guardsmen?” The lead guardsman replies, “Well, he was the best of us, and he doesn’t need any protection, nor does he want it.” The lead guardsman then orders the security to summon all the guardsmen and return the security guards to their posts. “We’re heading back to the palace,” he informs.

Meanwhile, at the palace, the Princess Ball is proceeding as planned. The Dweet brothers are mingling with the guests, and everyone is praising the Royal Family for their attire. The guardsmen return from Greater Landing and inform the head palace guardsman of the news. He finds Lizzes, and upon hearing the news, her eyes find the Dweet brothers. The brothers also lock eyes with the Duchess. The Duchess tells the guardsman not to worry about the brothers tonight. "We will deal with them in due time," she informs.

The brothers are very arrogant in their approach toward the guests, acting as if they are the center of attention. As Lizzes watches the brothers, the Queen is watching her. At that time, the palace guardsman announces, "Ladies and gentlemen, may I have your attention. We have a special surprise for the Royal Family." The family looks at each other, trying to figure out what the surprise is. The palace guardsman continues, "Ladies and gentlemen, I would like to introduce to you the first female guardsman." At that moment, the Royal Family stands up, and the guardsman exclaims, "Darlene!!!"

◆◆◆

CHAPTER 39

DARLENE RETURNS

Darlene steps into the room from behind the curtain. The guests whisper among themselves, "She's a guardsman? How, what's so special about her?" Some of the guests are laughing. Darlene wears the female guardsman super suit, but the guests don't know it because it looks like a regular dress to them. The Royal Family and the palace employees are the only ones clapping. The family doesn't know what is going to happen next, but they are all feeling a little sad for Darlene due to the guests' negative reactions, all except Lizzes. Darlene begins to make her way towards the Royal Family's table to acknowledge them.

The Dweet brothers, who will seize any opportunity to embarrass the family, step up towards Darlene and taunt, "Guardsmen, are you kidding me?" the palace guardsmen are ready to get involved, but Lizzes shakes them off. Then, the brothers make a crucial mistake. They step within two feet of a guardsman's space.

The space limit is three feet. Anything closer, and the guardsmen switch to self-defense mode. At that moment, Darlene steps back and activates her super suit. The suit turns into a pantsuit with a long-hooded cape that covers the suit. The suit's mask covers Darlene's face up to the eyes. The hood automatically positions itself over Darlene's head. The entire suit is sand brown in color. The lady's dress heel can transform into a fighting boot, and it's also sand brown. It takes only three seconds for the suit to activate into form. Guests are stunned as the glasses fall out of their hands, hitting the floor and shattering. Darlene spins so fast that her cape covers both the Dweet brothers. As the cape covers them, Darlene knocks out both of them!

When the cape uncovers the brothers, they both fall to the floor unconscious. Darlene spins and is now standing straight up with her cape completely covering her and the suit. The guests are utterly shocked. The King remarks to the Queen, "I don't hear anyone laughing now." The Prince looks at Earl and whispers, "Holy Shit!" Lizzes directs two palace guardsmen to step in and take the brothers to the medical room and stay there until they wake up. Lizzes walks up to Darlene, who is still wrapped up in her cape. She instructs Darlene to deactivate the suit. Lizzes steps back as Darlene deactivates the suit. The suit transforms back into the dress. Then Lizzes looks at her, gives her the biggest hug, and whispers, "You did it!!" Both of them smile. The entire Royal Family comes forward and gives her a hug. The Queen is the last to hug her. The Queen steps back and exclaims, "You are amazing!! I am proud of you." Then, the Queen addresses the guests, "Ladies and gentlemen, Darlene, the first female guardsman!!" The guests erupt in cheers and applause.

The King proposes a toast to Darlene. Everyone lifts their glasses, exclaiming, "To Darlene!" Darlene, who hasn't said a word to anyone yet, leans toward Lizzes and inquires, "How long do I have to stay here? I haven't seen my kids yet." Lizzes responds, "You mean to tell me that you came straight here from the training facility?" Darlene confirms, "Yes, I did. Didn't you know about this?" Lizzes replies, "No! Whose idea was it?" Darlene reveals, "The Queen's!!" Lizzes remarks, "Oh! Well, nothing I can do about that, but you can leave anytime you want." Darlene decides, "I'll stay another 10 minutes." Lizzes agrees, "Ok, but we need to talk about your living arrangements." Darlene acknowledges, "Ok." As they mingle through the crowd, Darlene spots her former coworkers from the Royal clothing store walking towards her. Vivian, Josephine, and Alicia approach Darlene and ask, "How do you feel? How does the suit feel? Do we need to make any adjustments?" They walk around Darlene, examining the suit as they ask their questions. Darlene assures them, "Ladies, the suit feels fine."

Then she expresses, "I want to thank you again for taking care of my kids. I don't know how I will ever repay you for that." The three ladies reply, “It was a pleasure taking care of those kids; they will be very happy to see you.” Vivian explains, “They are at my house with my kids and four guardsmen.” She adds, “But before you leave, we have a new wardrobe for you that will be delivered to your house.” Darlene guesses, “Let me guess, they are all super suits?” Vivian confirms, “Yes. Lizzes wants you to be ready for anything at all times. We even made one for you to sleep in.” Darlene chuckles, remarking, “You ladies have thought of everything.” Lizzes assures Darlene, “Yes, we have, and you are a very important part of my plan.” Darlene inquires, “I understand that, but who were those arrogant men?” Lizzes explains, “Those two men are very angry with me, so they are trouble. But don’t worry about them for now.”

Now, the King makes his way to Darlene. As they both look at each other in the eyes, the King admits, “I doubted you. I thought you would die doing the training, but you didn’t. I owe you an apology.” Darlene responds gratefully, “Thank you, Sir! I really appreciate that.” The King gives her another hug before leaving. While Darlene and Lizzes are walking around the room having short conversations with everyone, the Dweet brothers finally wake up in the medical room. They query the two guardsmen, “What happened?” The guardsman, smiling, explains, “You got too close to the female guardsman, and she did what she was trained to do.” The brothers recount, “I remember now, but she moved with super speed, and her dress changed into something out of this world. The next thing I remember is waking up in here." The brothers demand to go back into the ballroom, but the guardsmen escort them out of the palace, wishing them to get good rest for the rest of their night. As the brothers depart, they mutter to each other, "We must find out who made those suits." Back at the ballroom, Darlene announces, "It's time for me to go." Lizzes agrees, "Ok, but let's meet at the coffee shop in three days to discuss your living arrangements since you are a guardsman now." Darlene nods in agreement. Lizzes instructs four guardsmen to escort the coworkers and Darlene home. Darlene bids the Royal Family goodnight and leaves the palace.

As all the guests are leaving, the family gathers in the dining room. They all sit down and exchange looks for about 10 seconds. Breaking the silence, the Princess remarks with relief, "Well, thank God she didn't kill both of those men because she easily could have." As they all laugh, the Queen compliments Lizzes, "Those coworkers and that blacksmith of yours are simply remarkable at what they do. I want round-the-clock security along with all of their family members. Make sure that it is taken care of immediately. The last thing we need is for them to get kidnapped." Lizzes assures, "I will take care of that, Your Majesty." Earl inquires, "Lizzes, do those suits increase a person's strength?" Lizzes replies, "At least five times the strength of that person." She adds, "I don't know for sure, but I will find out from the ladies tomorrow if they have all that information. But I know for sure that the cape is bulletproof."

The King exclaims, "It is!!! The entire material is made up of steel dust particles. It's been tested by the ladies and the blacksmith within a 5 feet radius. The bullets made some dents at 5 feet, but anything outside of 5 feet, didn't leave even a scratch." The Prince remarks, "Holy shit!!" but immediately apologizes for his language. He continues, "Did you see how the people were looking at Darlene like she was some type of superhero?" The Princess interrupts, "I want one of those suits!!" The Queen glances at her with a serious look. The Princess, trying to handle the situation, replies, "Just kidding!!" The Queen directs, "Lizzes, I want Darlene to start her daily four-hours-a-day training with the three Chinese as soon as possible." Lizzes responds, "I will give her four or five days to spend with her children and to visit her aunts, uncles, grandmother, and cousins. Then, I will get her started. The Chinese will begin constructing their training facility tomorrow. They should have it ready for training in a couple of days. Then, we will get the 20 guardsmen started with their training. Plus, we have 100 of the super suits ready in all four colors, with another 100 ready in 2 months."

The Queen expresses enthusiasm, "Great! Tomorrow, let's get the 20 guardsmen training in those suits." Lizzes inquires, "Your majesty, may I make a suggestion, please?" The Queen approves, "Of course." Lizzes proposes, "The guardsmen are already superb fighters. Maybe we should just train them on how to use the suits for a couple of days and send them to France." She adds, "Darlene learned how to use her suit in less than two hours. When they get back, they can start their training with the Chinese men." The King agrees, "It's a good idea those five men need to be caught." The Queen affirms, "Agreed. Make it happen. I'm tired." She gets up, bids goodnight, and retires to her room. The King also bids, "Good night." Then, the rest of the Royal Family makes their way to their rooms. Later that night, Lizzes has another dream.

◆◆◆

CHAPTER 40

DREAM OF THE FUTURE

That night, God gives Lizzes another dream. She envisions her four-time great niece, Princess Stacy, engaged in martial arts sparring with seven of her guardsmen in World City, Puerto Rico. Princess Stacy wears a skintight outfit that's all black. It has a long, hooded black cape and has the capability of blending into any object. Lizzes observes that Princess Stacy jumps onto the wall and disappears. Then, she leaps from the wall, lands on the floor, and vanishes. Launching off the floor, she performs two flips in the air, and then she disengages the cape, which turns into six separate capes.

Now Princess Stacy and her six capes are facing all seven guardsmen and are in fighting stances. She is now in a tight, light brown suit with a cape that looks exactly like a lioness. The capes are in 6 different colors and are armed with enough weapons and ammo to take down 500 men. They begin to fight. The capes and

Princess Stacy each engage the guardsmen using fourteen different kung fu styles. Lizzes notices a clock on the wall displaying February 24th, 2022. They remain in action for about 10 minutes, then three scientists from the top floor of the practice room declare, "Time," prompting everyone to stop fighting. The scientist instructs Princess Stacy to engage the cape. She activates the cape through mind control, and all seven capes, including the lioness cape, transform back to the black cape and engage itself back onto Princess Stacy's black suit. The three scientists make their way into the practice room.

Lizzes reads the name tags of all three scientists. Each scientist shares the same last name as her blacksmith, Mr. Davids. Then Lizzes sees three ladies come into the room, all with the first names of her coworkers: Vivian, Alicia, and Josephine. The scientists examine Princess Stacy while the women inspect the suit. While Princess Stacy is being examined, two of her world intelligence leaders enter the room. One wears a Russian General uniform, and the other one has a Ukrainian General uniform. They both just stand there. Lizzes observes that Princess Stacy glances at the two Generals and commands everyone to stop the examinations and testing.

She walks up to the Generals. The Ukrainian General announces, "Princess, you are needed in the World Leaders Conference Room." She follows them into the room along with her seven female lioness guardsmen, each with a female lion and seven panther guardsmen, each partnered with a black panther. These are her personal bodyguards. Upon entering the conference room, all her world intelligence leaders rise to their feet—two hundred of them representing nearly every country. Lizzes watches Princess Stacy walk to the front of the room and gaze at the big screen TV. Lizzes can see the anger and frustration on Princess Stacy's face, but she can't see what it is on the screen. Lizzes overhears Princess Stacy instruct her intelligence leaders to inform both presidents to make sure that all civilians have safe passageways for their safety, and if anyone wants to leave or come to any city in the world, they can! Without interference from either country. Then she hears the Princess declare, "If these demands are not met by both presidents, we will make sure the demands are kept by all means necessary!"

Then she hears the Princess command, "Get me the president of the United States on screen." Lizzes sees the Princess turn to the left and is now looking right at her and smiles. Now, Lizzes observes the Princess walking towards her as if she can see her. The Princess extends her hand towards Lizzes. One of Princess Stacy's lioness guardsmen inquires, "Princess, are you ok?" The Princess doesn't respond. Then Lizzes wakes up. She sits up, drenched in a cold sweat. Earl awakens and questions, "Are you ok?" Lizzes replies, "I just had the weirdest dream. I saw our 4th great-granddaughter, and her name is Princess Stacy."

"She is beautiful!" Lizzes exclaims, beginning to cry, and continues to assure Earl, "I'm not crazy, but I think she saw me, and she reached out her hand towards me." Earl advises, "Write it down now while it's fresh in your head. We will get the artist to draw up a sketch of Princess Stacy in the morning." Lizzes writes down the dream.

She lies back down and starts to dream once more. This time, Princess Stacy is in her room, looking up at the ceiling, and she sees Lizzes! She reaches up and calls out, "Grandmother Lizzes, can you see and hear me?" Lizzes responds eagerly, "Yes!!!"

"Princess," Lizzes questions, tears streaming from both of them, "But how is this possible?" The Princess admits, "I don't know, but I've wished many nights that I could just talk to you. Just to hear your voice and to see your face." The Princess reaches out her hand to Lizzes. Lizzes reaches back, but their hands pass through each other. The Princess responds, "Grandmother, I think you are in a deep sleep." Lizzes exclaims, "But I can hear and see you!! We're having a conversation." The Princess shoots back, "Yes! You're dreaming, but somehow, you have connected telepathically with me here in the future." Then she inquires, "Grandmother, have you connected with anyone else in the family?" Lizzes confirms, "No! Just you, granddaughter."

Both the Princess and Lizzes are crying uncontrollably. Lizzes instructs, "I have to go now, but I want you to tell the family of what you have witnessed here, ok?" The Princess vows, "I will, great-grandmother, I promise!" Lizzes asks the Princess, "Do you see this picture on the wall?" The Princess exclaims, "Yes!! I have that picture!! When I look closely at that picture, it says a lot without saying anything." Lizzes assures, "I love you, Princess, and I will be seeing you again soon." The Princess responds, "I love you too, grandmother," with that Lizzes fade away! Then she wakes up again to find Earl standing over her, shaking her awake. Earl exclaims, "Lizzes!! I've been trying to wake you for 5 minutes now! I'm calling the doctor!" Lizzes reassures, "No, Earl, I'm fine. I was having a conversation with Princess Stacy again." Earl questions, "Again?" Lizzes marvels, "Yes! I don't know why this is happening, but it's amazing some of the things I've seen talking to her." Earl inquires, "Did you see the year?" Lizzes confirms, "Yes, February 2022." Earl blurts out, "Holy shit!!!" Lizzes acknowledges, "Yeah, it's a strong connection." Earl instructs, "Ok, write down what happened, and get dressed. I'm excited to read what you see." Lizzes writes everything down. She arrives at the breakfast table and takes a seat. She states, "I have something I want you to hear."

Lizzes begins to read her dreams to the family. They are all stunned! They are completely shocked after Lizzes tells them about Princess Stacy's suit and how it's advanced. The Princess, like the

Queen, is crying and extremely emotional. The Queen inquires, "What does she look like?" Lizzes responds, "She's beautiful with long, jet-black curly hair." The Princess exclaims, "God really loves you, Lizzes!" Lizzes affirms, "He loves all of us. That's why we must vow to do right by Him." In that moment, Lizzes feels a strong urgency to pray. She urges everyone to join hands. Lizzes starts her prayer. After the prayer, Lizzes declares, "Let's all, from this day forward, vow to be here for the welfare, peace, and protection of all people that are in need." From that moment on, the family made a vow to help all the people. No matter what race, religion, or country they come from.

CHAPTER 41

THE PANTHER GUARDSMEN

That morning after breakfast Lizzes, Earl, the Princess, and the Prince, along with 7 of the Royal guardsmen, who are now wearing and have had a couple of days training on the blue super suits, went to pick up the three Chinese men and take them to Greater Landing to see their new training facility. But little do they know they are being followed by two men on horseback. The Dweet brothers had hired these two men to spy on the guardsmen. They want to know who made those suits. As the Family reaches the hotel, the lead guardsman spots the two spies and alerts Lizzes. She instructs the guardsmen to go as planned but keeps an eye on them. They pick up the Chinese men and head towards Greater Landing.

One of the Chinese men, Wong, asks Lizzes, "So what is the story with those men who wanted to attack the city of Greater Landing but were told not to by the tall, big man?" A puzzled look crosses Lizzes' face. She questions, "How do you know this? And what tall, big man?" Wong replies, "The alleys echo at night." Lizzes explains, "Well, I don't know what that means. But there are two brothers. Their names are Jeff and John Dweet. They had the leases of 21 black-owned businesses in Greater Landing and were overpricing the black business owners. So, when all their leases were up for renewal, the business owners signed with us instead of the Dweet brothers. Then, we came to find out the Dweet brothers lied to the black business owners about owning all of the buildings and threatened to throw them out if they didn't pay the increased rent. We found out the city of Greater Landing owned the buildings, and the brothers were just leasing the buildings from the city."

She continues, "So, before the brothers' leases with the city were up for renewal, we signed new leases for the 21 buildings with the city, and now the brothers have no valued interest in Greater Landing. We also own 15 other buildings in Greater Landing, which are now being developed into apartments, grocery stores, clothing stores, and lots more. We have also got authorization from the city to put a ten-foot fence around the Greater Landing with four entryways in and out of the city." Wong nods and responds, "So, the brothers are very angry with you?" Lizzes confirms, "Extremely!! But we have our eyes on them." Wong counters, "As they also have eyes on you." When they reach the east entranceway, the Chinese men observe four black security guards and two guardsmen positioned inside. And there are two ten-foot huts on both of their sides—one for entering and the other for exiting. The huts, twenty feet apart, are connected by a walkway on top. Each contains a stairway inside to reach the top.

The security guards do their checks and allow the horse and carriage to enter. The Chinese men express their admiration. They enter Greater Landing; the Chinese men immediately notice all the construction and the changed atmosphere. Wong notes, "There are a lot of black people here." Smiling, Lizzes explains, "Greater Landing is 95% black populated. Lots are from Africa. You're very safe here." As they arrive at the training facility, the Chinese men observe that it's located in the back of the city of about two blocks, isolated and enclosed by bricks. They step into the building, which has been completely remodeled, with their living quarters on the first floor, separate from the training area. It's also surrounded by homeless people, causing concern among the Chinese men.

They inquire, "Why are those homeless people here? Can we move them somewhere else in the city?" Lizzes replies with a smile, "Those homeless people are our city spies called WOTS, word on the street."Then she goes on to explain, "What you are seeing now is them getting prepared to go out into the city of London, Greater Landing, Manchester, and other surrounding cities. They hang out in alleys and other parts of the cities and listen to people talk. No one would suspect a homeless person as a spy. But, if it makes you gentlemen uncomfortable, I can have them prepare somewhere else." The Chinese men gather for a discussion. They then agree to let them stay where they are. After that, they walk up to the 4th floor and back down to the first floor. They engage in another discussion.

Wong states, "Every level will have to be painted certain colors and the stairs leading to every level also." Lizzes responds, "Ok, we can get that taken care of as soon as possible." They request to see the yard and when they enter it, they observe 14 black security guards fixing up the backyard, which is about 3 acres. Lizzes points out, "You see those gentlemen? I want them to be your first students. There is going to be one part of the Royal Family's personal security guards called 'The Panther Guardsmen.' But there is one small problem." Wong exclaims, "Problem!!" Lizzes confirms, "Yes." She then instructs the guardsmen to bring out 14 black panther cubs. They are about one month old.

All the security guards rush over to see the cubs with smiles on their faces. Lizzes explains, "The problem is the security guards will have to be trained by you, and they also have to train their black panther cub. The cubs and the security guards will have to stay here in the joining building next door." The Chinese men are stunned. They question, "How did you get 14 black panther cubs?" Lizzes reveals, "They were imported from Africa. They had two sets of mothers who were killed by poachers. The poachers gathered the cubs and were going to sell them separately. One of our close allies arrested the men and found the cubs. The Allies asked around to see if anyone wanted to take on the responsibility of raising the cubs. We were the first ones they got in contact with."

The Chinese men acknowledge that it will be challenging for them to train themselves and the cubs at the same time. Those cubs must not only stay with them 24/7, but they also have to be with them and the family on a daily basis. Wong asks, "Is the Royal Family prepared to spend time with the cubs for at least an hour of your day so that the cubs will get acquainted with you?" The family agrees, "Yes, but the cubs, for one hour a day, will have to be brought to the palace so they can get acquainted with everyone there every day." Wong responds, "Agreed!" Lizzes then turns to address all the security guards. She declares, "Each cub that you have is your responsibility now. They all have collars with their names. You will be here for an entire year of training with these men. You will live here. So, after today, go home and tell your families what you will be doing. You are not security guards anymore; you are 'The Panther Guardsmen,' part of the Royal Family's personal security guards."

She then directs guardsmen to bring the 14 Panther super suits. Lizzes states, "Tomorrow morning, meet here. You will be trained on how to use these suits 2 hours a day for seven weeks by Vivian, who is one of the designers of the suit, starting from tomorrow morning at 10 am." Lizzes looks at the security guards and offers,

"If any of you want to back out, this is your time to do so and remain a security guard. Step forward!" No one steps forward. Lizzes approves, "Good! Finish what you are doing here today, go home, and return tomorrow." Then she announces, "Mr Wong, they're all yours." Lizzes and the family shake hands with all the men and head back to the nonprofit, 'Blessed the People Foundation.' As the family arrives at the nonprofit, they see the ladies have hired extra help and are serving food to the homeless and residents around the city of Greater Landing. They also observe the first signs of the roads being paved for the automobile. There are between seven and eight hundred automobiles in the country. Lizzes predicts, "Pretty soon, there will be only automobiles in this city. I want to eliminate the smell of horse waste in this city."

As the family leaves the nonprofit, which is a block away from the east entrance, they see the two spies following them at the entrance. Lizzes has informed the security guards and the two guardsmen of the situation, instructing them to deny the spies entry into Greater Landing. At that moment, the Prince and the Princess notice a tall figure walking towards them. The tall figure yells their names! Lizzes asks, "Who is that?" The Prince starts running towards the tall figure, and the guardsmen run after the Prince.

CHAPTER 42

FRIENDS FOR LIFE

As the Prince is running towards the tall figure, with the guardsmen chasing after him, Lizzes and Earl are wondering who it is the Prince is running towards. Lizzes questions the Princess, "Who is that?" The Princess reveals, "It is Prince Edward Williamson. He is the Prince's first cousin. He's been away for five years. We didn't know he was back in town." Lizzes comments, "He must be the tall guy that the Chinese men were talking about." As the Prince and Mr Williamson greet each other, Lizzes notices that the Princess isn't as thrilled as the Prince.

Lizzes inquires of the Princess, "Is everything ok?" The Princess responds ambiguously, "Yes and no! The Prince was devastated when Prince Edward went away. Those two grew up together and did everything together. To make matters worse, Prince Edward wanted no visitors when he was incarcerated. So, the Prince hasn't seen him in 5 years." Lizzes probes, "What did he do to get incarcerated?" The Princess explains, "He doesn't like authority or like being told what to do, so he went down a dark path that we all tried to prevent him from going. But there was nothing we could do. His mind was made up. I just don't want the Prince to go through that again." The Prince is now on his way back to the family with Mr Williamson.

The Prince announces, "Lizzes, Earl, let me introduce you to my cousin, Prince Edward Williamson. Prince Edward Williamson, this is Duchess and Duke Lizzes and Earl Melvin." They exchange greetings. The Princess is less enthusiastic in her greeting. She walks up to Prince Williamson. She stares at him with an angry look. Nobody is saying a word! The Princess states, "My husband was devastated when you left us. But his heart was crushed when you refused to have visitation from your family, especially him. I had to deal with his heartache. You were brothers, and he loved you like one. I refuse to have you just pop up and think everything is ok!" A dead silence ensues.

Prince Williamson acknowledges, "I completely understand. At that time, I was embarrassed and ashamed and didn't want my family to see me like that. I'm sorry that I hurt my family. It was a very difficult five-year period. But, during that time, I grew up a lot. I realized what everyone was trying to tell me back then. I hope that one day, my family can forgive me for all the hurt and pain that I've inflicted on my family." The Princess takes a step towards Prince Williamson. She warns, "We have forgiven you a long time ago, but if you hurt my husband again, I'm going to rip your heart out and stuff it back down your throat!! I don't care how big and tall you are. Do we have an understanding?" Prince Williamson concedes, "Yes! I understand." The Princess probes, "Now, why haven't you stopped by the palace and visited the King and Queen?" Prince Williamson admits, "I'm embarrassed and scared a little. I'm not ready to face them yet. I promise I will stop by when I feel that I'm ready." The Princess looks at Prince Williamson and retorts, "Nonsense!!"

She commands her Royal Guardsmen to escort the Prince and Prince Williamson to the palace in the royal carriage of the Princess and Prince. She gets into Lizzes and Earl's royal carriage. She also instructs the guardsmen to ensure he doesn't attempt to flee. Two guardsmen position themselves beside Prince Williamson, smiling as they know he's scared to death. Prince Williamson climbs into the royal carriage alongside the Prince. He feels more nervous than ever before. He looks at the Prince, who is sweating heavily.

The Prince advises Mr. Williamson to calm down. "It's going to be ok; look at the bright side. They will be happy to see you, but they're also going to see where your head's at. So relax and prepare yourself," he suggests. Prince Williamson closes his eyes and takes a couple of deep breaths while the guardsmen and the Prince smile at each other. The Prince cautions Prince Williamson, “And, oh yeah, please don’t try anything stupid like trying to run or fight any of the guardsmen like you did five years ago. A lot has changed. See those suits the guardsmen are wearing?” Prince Williamson acknowledges, “Yes, I notice them.” The Prince details, “Well, their super suits are equipped with enough weaponry to take down 100 men, and they increase the guardsmen’s strength ten times that of the average man.” Mr Williamson wears a stunned expression on his face. He exclaims, “Those suits!!!? They look like regular suits with an upgrade.” The Prince has seen that look in Mr Williamson’s eyes before. The Prince warns, “Edward, just don’t! I know that look, so don’t even think about trying one of the guardsmen.” One of the guardsmen pleads, “Please don’t. You wouldn’t last five seconds.” Mr. Williamson turns to the Prince and asserts, “What??!! I’m not going to try anything. Everyone relax.” The Prince just shakes his head.

Meanwhile, Lizzes, Earl, and the Princess arrive at the home of one of the young black men who was shot by the five white men and has taken up residence in France. Earl knocks on the door, which both young men open with a smile, inviting Lizzes, the Princess, and Earl inside. One young man looks at the guardsmen stationed outside and comments, “Nice suits.” Both the young men’s mothers then enter the room. They invite the Royal Family to have a seat. One of the mothers gets right to the point and asks, “So, do you have any information on the men who shot our son?" Lizzes assures, "We do. We know exactly where they're located and I promise you, we will bring them to justice." The mother remarks, "Ok, but that's not why you are here," as she looks at the family. Lizzes responds, "No, it is not. We are here to offer your sons an opportunity." The mother echoes, "Opportunity? I don't mean to disrespect you, but the last opportunity you offered our sons almost got them killed!" Lizzes acknowledges, "I completely understand your concern, as I was concerned also."

The mother exclaims, "Was!!!" Lizzes clarifies, "I was concerned, but not anymore." She then proposes, "I want to offer your sons a chance to train as my personal security guards called 'the Panther Guardsmen.' I promise you, after they are trained, no one in their right mind will think about doing them any harm." One of the mothers inquires, "Can you guarantee that?" Lizzes confirms, "Yes." Then, she invites one of the guardsmen inside. She requests one of the sons to remove the coffee table and directs everyone to stand back. She orders the guardsmen to activate the suit. The guardsmen activate the suit, and it changes from light sky blue to dark blue. Lizzes has implemented a hooded cap onto the men's super-suit just like the female super-suit. The mothers appear frightened, while the two young men are clearly fascinated.

Lizzes explains the weapons that are on the suit to the young men and their mothers. Then, she instructs the guardsmen to deactivate the suit. The suit returns to a regular men's suit. Lizzes turns to the mothers and expresses, "I would love for your sons to be trained and be a part of our personal security force." The mothers remain frightened but realize that if their sons join this elite force, they will be able to fight against racism in the black community and around the world. The mothers ask the sons, "What do you want to do?"

Both men, at the same time, declare, "I'm in!!!!" The mothers consent, "Okay." One mother tells Lizzes, "We are worried and counting on you to protect our sons." Lizzes assures, "Ma'am, I guarantee you that once your sons are on the training, they will not need any protection from anyone." Then, she instructs the sons to be ready in the morning. "A guardsman will come to pick you up." She approaches both mothers and states, "Your sons will be trained at our new facility in this city. They will be trained for one year and live on the facility grounds. I will get you a visitation schedule as soon as possible." Lizzes expresses to the mothers, "Thank you for allowing your sons to do this. Those two young men hold a special place in our hearts after what they've been through." The Royal Family hugs the mother and the two sons, then exits the home.

CHAPTER 43

BETRAY ARE NOT TO BETRAY

As the family leaves Greater Landing, they pass by the Greater Landing Church. They hear music and someone singing. The music sounds so beautiful and peaceful that Lizzes instructs the guardsmen to stop. She wants to enter the church. The guardsmen stop, the four enter the church, and everyone inside stops what they're doing. Then, the family enters. The people in the church all start whispering to each other, "It's the Royal Family. That's Lizzes, the Princess, and Earl." Then Lizzes urges, "Please, please don't stop singing. We heard you from the outside, and you sound so beautiful. Do you mind if we sit and listen?"

The black lead female singer replies, "Of course not! We are excited to have you here, and it would be a pleasure and an honor to sing while you hear us." The music begins to play—the drums, piano, organ, and bass guitar are all in tune. Then, the choir begins to sing. The Princess leans over to Lizzes and muses, "I don't know what angels sound like singing, but it must sound like this." Lizzes confides in the Princess, "I know, I've never heard anything like this." Lizzes glances at Earl and is going to ask him what he thinks, but seeing the tears coming down his face, she just grabs his hand and says nothing. After the choir finishes singing, something amazing occurs! The air fills with sounds of "Hallelujah" and "Thank you, Jesus!" The Holy Spirit has shown and has touched the Royal Family. Lizzes is now speaking in a different language that she cannot control. The Princess and Earl are crying their eyes out, exclaiming, "Thank you, Jesus!" over and over again! The people in the church begin running and dancing all over the church.

Once everything calms down, the lead singer, Karen Moss, walks up to the Royal Family and informs them that God has anointed them to do His work. Then, turning to Lizzes, she adds, "But you, because of you, your family will prosper for all eternity." Then, she begins to pray for the Royal Family. After the prayer, Lizzes inquires, "What time is your Sunday service." Karen responds, "Every Sunday at 11 am." Lizzes confirms, "See you on Sunday." After they leave and enter London, Lizzes spots her three co-workers with Darlene walking into the candy store. They leave their guardsmen outside the candy store since Darlene is with them.

Then they notice the Dweet brothers walking into the soda shop, which is next door and has walk-in access to the candy shop. Lizzes orders her guardsmen to stop and says that she wants to observe this situation. Lizzes is also aware that Darlene has a very short fuse. While outside the candy shop, Lizzes coworker's guardsmen are now on alert as they have also seen the Dweet brothers enter the soda shop next door. The Princess questions, "What do you think Darlene will do if the brothers approach her?" With nervousness in her voice, Lizzes admits, "I don't know. Darlene is frightening when she is in guardsmen mode, and quite frankly, she scares me a little cause I can't read her like the other guardsmen. She reasons after the fact." Earl muses, "I wonder how thick those windows are?"

Lizzes looks at Earl, then turns her gaze to the windows, noting his very serious expression. As the ladies are in the store buying candy, the brothers spot Darlene! Jeff Dweet exclaims to his brother, "John, John, look!! It's the lady from the Princess ball, Darlene! Do you think she's wearing that suit?" John responds, "I don't think so. That's a different dress from the one she had on at the Princess ball." John continues, "Even if she's not wearing the suit, she is still a guardsman, and what she did to us at the Princess ball shows she throws caution out the window, and that makes her very dangerous! If not the most dangerous guardsmen out of all of them. She reacts first and thinks later! But I don't care about any of that. It doesn't change my opinion about the guardsmen at all." Jeff concedes, "I know, but let's go apologize for our actions at the ball." John declares arrogantly, "I'm not apologizing for anything. We did nothing wrong; she attacked us." John inquires of Jeff, "Do you have your gun?"

Jeff retorts, "Are you crazy?!! There are four guardsmen outside that window. If we threaten her, they will most definitely kill us or seriously hurt us. Let's go and apologize. Put your pride aside!! And stop talking stupid!!!" Jeff proceeds to walk towards Darlene to apologize. As he approaches the ladies, the guardsmen outside begin to watch closely. Their focus is not on the ladies or Darlene's well-being but on the brother's well-being. The guardsmen know that Darlene is dynamite, ready to be ignited and explode. Jeff makes his way to the ladies as his brother stays still. Darlene and the ladies notice him and Darlene becomes agitated and nearly activates her suit. But she stops as Jeff takes off his hat. He greets them, "Excuse me, ladies, my name is Jeff Dweet." He smiles at Darlene and remarks, "We have already met." He continues, "I mean no disrespect. I just came over to apologize, for my brother and I disrespected you, Darlene, at the night of the Princess ball. It was just a shock to us and everyone that a lady made it through the guardsmen training."

Darlene responds, "Well, I accept your apology, but I know who you and your brother are and what you're trying to do to Lizzes and the guardsmen. You and your brother better tread lightly." Jeff acknowledges, "You are right! We do have a vendetta against the duchess and the guardsmen, but this isn't about that. This is about the disrespect we showed you at the Princess ball." Darlene asserts, "As long as we have an understanding." Jeff confirms, "Yes, we have an understanding," and begins to walk away. Darlene interjects, "Excuse me, we have an understanding, but what about your brother? He's sitting over there with that same disrespectful look he had at the Princess ball." Jeff explains, "He's still upset about the situation with the Duchess. I'm trying to separate the two." Darlene remarks, "I'm ok with you because you're honest about everything but your brother…!!"

Watching them from a distance, John can tell they are talking about him; he stands up with an attitude written all over his posture. He advances towards his brother and the ladies and states, "So we meet again. Listen, I don't care what my brother told you. I'm not agreeing to it. I don't care if you are a guardsman! Now go tell that to your Master!!" He then commands, "Let's go, Jeff!" Jeff looks at his brother with a surprised look as he walks away. When he turns around, he sees that Darlene has activated her super suit. Jeff is scared to death because he didn't know that she was wearing a suit, and so are the ladies.

They know Darlene is out to earn her guardsmen's respect by all means necessary. Darlene jumps in the air and across the room about ten feet, turns a flip, and lands directly in front of John Dweet. John is afraid but doesn't care. Darlene asserts, "You have 3 seconds to apologize for that Master comment!" The guardsmen outside see everything as John Dweet turns his nose up to Darlene and tries to walk away. The guardsmen rush in, but before they get to her, Darlene grabs John from behind and throws him towards a window. The window is blocked by two guardsmen who instinctively know how to block it. But she has so much force that both the guardsmen and John Dweet go flying through the window!! John lands on top of the guardsmen, who are not hurt that badly. The other two guardsmen activate their suits in order to calm down Darlene. Darlene leaps over them and through the window, aiming to reach John Dweet, who is just picking himself up off of the guardsmen. Darlene seizes John Dweet with one hand and lifts him high above her head, getting ready to throw him again. The two guardsmen dive at Darlene and try to tackle her, but she jumps high in the air with John still above her head. The guardsmen miss her, rolling over to land on their feet with one knee up and one knee on the ground. Their left hand is also on the ground in a football stance, ready to attack again.

Immediately, Lizzes and the Royal Family run towards the scene, screaming, “Darlene, stop!!!” Lizzes’ coworkers also come running out of the store, echoing, “Darlene, stop!!” Darlene turns to Lizzes and drops John face-first on the ground. The two guardsmen on the ground are now up and getting ready to activate their super suits, but Lizzes stops them. Jeff helps his brother to his feet while Darlene turns her attention back to him. The two guardsmen who activated their suits are now in a position to take Darlene down. Lizzes leaps in front of Darlene and cries out, "Darlene, no!!!" Darlene's gaze remains fixed on John.

Lizzes shouts at Jeff, "Get your brother out of here. Now!!!" Jeff seizes his brother, cursing as he drags him away, "You freaking idiot! What the hell is wrong with you?" Darlene's eyes are focused on John like a pit bull. Once the brothers disappear around the corner, Darlene relaxes and deactivates the suit. There is also a relief on the guardsmen's faces. Lizzes inquires of Darlene, "What happened there that would send you in a rage like that?" Darlene declares, "John Dweet is trouble!!! And very disrespectful, and I'm not taking any disrespect from anyone!! Don't underestimate him!! He won't stop until he destroys you and the guardsmen. But his brother Jeff is the total opposite. He was very apologetic and respectful. I don't like John Dweet one bit!!!!"

Lizzes looks at the ladies, who all nod in agreement with Darlene. Josephine can see Darlene is breathing a little heavily. She checks her pulse and heart rate. Josephine announces, "Your blood pressure is high." She advises Darlene, "You cannot go into a rage like that again until we make some adjustments to the suits to fix the high blood pressure issue." Darlene responds, "Ok, but I can't promise you it that will not happen again if I see him." Lizzes looks at the ladies and directs, "Fix that immediately!!!" Then she looks at Darlene and asks, "Are you ok now?" Darlene assures, "Yes, I'm fine." Lizzes reminds, "Ok. Remember tomorrow we have a meeting at the coffee shop, ok?" Lizzes is trying to change the subject so that Darlene can shift her mind to think about something else. Darlene agrees, "Ok."

Lizzes instructs a guardsman to take care of the damages. Then, she instructs her coworker's guardsmen to escort the ladies home. One guardsman comments, "Duchess, we don't think Darlene needs an escort home. It would take a completely idiotic, crazy person to approach her with any wrongdoing in mind." Lizzes asserts, "Exactly!! That's why I need you to escort her home for the safety of others." One of the guardsmen walks up to Darlene, peers into her eyes, then taps her on the head and jests, "Darlene, are you in there?" Darlene retorts, "Oh, stop it!!" And she walks away. The others burst into laughter.

Now, Lizzes looks around and notices the crowd that is watching everything and orders the guardsmen to disperse them. Then she screams Earl's name! Earl replies from the carriage, "I'm here, I'm in the carriage." Lizzes and the Princess walk back to the carriage. Lizzes questions Earl, "Why were you in the carriage when we were all trying to calm Darlene down?" Earl explains, "If a mosquito bites Darlene, she's going to activate that suit just to kill the mosquito! She would have killed that gentleman if the guardsmen weren't there. Nope! She scares the crap out of me! She's your problem, not mine!!"

The Princess begins to laugh. Earl cautions, "You better hope she never betrays you!" He then continues, "Can you imagine an army of angry, aggressive, and nonsense women like Darlene!! Did you see the guardsmen's eyes? They know she is a ticking bomb!! But you know what scares me about Darlene? When she hasn't activated that suit, she's this beautiful, calm woman! It's like two different people."

He suggests, "You need to develop a kill switch or something for her suits so you can deactivate her when she goes in a rage like that." Then he exclaims, "She didn't even use any weapons on the suit!!!"

Lizzes takes a deep breath and shoots back, "My Goodness!!!"

◆◆◆

CHAPTER 44

GET IT TOGETHER AND UNDER CONTROL

At the palace, the Prince and Mr Williamson arrive. The butler opens the door. The butler is delighted to see Mr Williamson. He greets him, "Well, well, it's been a long time, Prince Edward. How are you?" Prince Edward replies, "I'm doing good. Still adjusting, but I'm doing ok. Thank you for asking." The butler responds with a smile, "Glad to hear that." He informs them, "You two can wait in the Queen and King's study while I go to the palace garden and let them know they have a visitor." Once the butler departs, Prince Edward admits, "My heart is beating really fast."

Then, a female server with light brown skin brings in a plate of fruit for the two Princes to snack on. Prince Edward has his eyes locked on her as she is beautiful! As she leaves the room with a smile, the Prince watches Prince Edward's reaction. Prince Edward inquires, "Who is that?!!!" The Prince answers, "That the butler's niece, Briana, and she has a boyfriend. So don't even think about it 'cause the Queen loves her like a daughter and treats her that way." Prince Edward requests, "Introduce me to her." The Prince responds, "Did you hear a word I said?" Prince Edward asserts, "Yes, every word!" "So, are you going to introduce me to her?" The Prince agrees, "Ok, but don't try anything." Briana enters the room with beverages and places them on the table. She asks the Princes if they need anything else. The Prince responds, "No, Briana, thank you very much." He then introduces, "Briana, this is my cousin Prince Edward." Briana greets, "How do you do, Prince Edward?" to which the Prince replies, "I'm doing well." Then Prince Edward freezes for a second, and Briana remarks, "Well, it was nice meeting you, Prince Edward. Have a good day." As Briana exits the room, the Prince looks at Prince Edward and remarks, laughing hysterically, "You froze up like an ice cube!!"

Prince Edward exclaims, "I don't know what happened! She's so beautiful!" The Prince advises, "Well, she's taken, so get yourself together and under control." Meanwhile, the butler reaches the garden and announces, "Your Majesties, you have a guest in your study." The Queen and King look at each other. They can tell the guest is someone of importance from the way the butler is acting suspiciously. The Queen instructs, "Let the guest know we will be there in a few minutes." The butler walks back into the Queen's study and informs Prince Edward, "The Queen and King will be here in a few minutes," and then leaves the room.

Prince Edward confesses to the Prince, "I'm really nervous!" The Prince exclaims, "Good grief, get control of yourself. It's your aunt and uncle. You're acting like you have never met them before!!!" Then, the Queen and King walk in, and Prince Edward stands up. To his surprise, the King and Queen are excited to see him. The Queen exclaims joyfully at Edward, rushes to him, and gives him a hug. She says, "I'm so glad to see you! When did you get home?" Prince Edward looks at the Prince and replies, "Two weeks ago." They step back, now visibly upset! She inquires, "What!! You've been home for two weeks, and you didn't come to see us?" Prince Edward responds, "I'm sorry, but I was embarrassed! And ashamed." The Queen questions, "Why? We're your family. You should never be embarrassed or ashamed, no matter what. Your mother and father should have told us."

Prince Edward explains, "I asked them not to because I wanted to do it." The King interjects because he knows the Queen isn't going to let up. The King remarks, "Oh, give the lad a break. He's here now." He kindly moves the Queen to the side and then says warmly, "Edward, my boy, I'm glad to see you! You look good. Have a seat." Everyone takes a seat, then the Queen looks at the Prince and asks, "Wait a minute, where is your wife?" The Prince and Prince Edward exchange looks, and then he replies, “She’s with Earl and Lizzes.” The Queen repeats, puzzled, “Earl and Lizzes?” Confused, the King and Queen look at each other, and she then realizes, “Oh, I get it. You were told to come and visit by the Princess. She must have really let you have it.” Prince Edward agrees, “Yes, and then some…” Just then, the Princess, Lizzes, and Earl walk towards the Queen’s study. The Princess and Lizzes step in and acknowledge the Queen and King. The Princess looks at Prince Edward and teases, “I see you still alive.” The Prince bursts out laughing!

Lizzes says, “Pardon me, Your Majesty, but I’m tired, and it’s been a long day. I’m going to my room and rest before dinner.” The Princess adds, “I am also tired and need a nap.” The Queen notices that the ladies’ clothes are dirty. She asks, “Wait a minute, why are you so filthy?” Lizzes replies, “Your majesty, if you don’t mind, can I tell you during dinner?” The Queen agrees, “Ok, at dinner.” Lizzes and the Princess responds, “Thank you.” They then depart from the study. Earl stops by the bathroom and is now passing by the Queen’s study. The Queen calls out, “Earl, come here for a minute, please.” Earl enters the study, and the Queen inquires, “What’s going on with those two ladies?” Earl takes a deep breath, pauses for a second, and exclaims, “Darlene is freaking nuts!!! Lizzes needs to get her under control!!” He adds, “Excuse me,” and then exits the study. Now, everyone in the study is looking around at each other, trying to figure out what Darlene did. The Queen is too impatient to wait and instructs one of the palace guards, "Go find out what happened from Lizzes and Earl's guardsmen." The Prince stands and says, "Excuse me," and leaves to check on his wife. Prince Edward asks, "Who is Darlene?" The Queen explains, "There is a lot that has been changed since you have been gone. Darlene is our first female guardsman." Prince Edward exclaims, "What?!!! A female guardsman? You're kidding, right?" The King remarks, "No! She's serious!" At that moment, one of Lizzes' guardsmen walks into the study. The Queen inquires, "What happened with Darlene today?" One of the guardsmen explains, "Well, to make a long story short, John Dweet was disrespectful to Darlene at the candy store, and she attacked him. Two guardsmen activated the suits and tried to take her down in order to control her, but she was too strong, too quick, and too fast for them. If Lizzes wasn't there, she would have killed him. She hates John Dweet! Her anger and attitude make her almost unstoppable."

Prince Edward is in disbelief and exclaims, "This is hard to believe. I must see this for myself." The King cautions, "Edward, please don't try anything stupid." Then he informs the Queen, "Lizzes must get Darlene under control." Prince Edward announces, "Well, if you don't mind, I'm going to call it a night." The King reminds Prince Edward, "Nothing stupid." The Prince smiles, embraces the Queen with a hug, and bids, "Goodnight." That night at dinner, Lizzes and the Princess appear really exhausted. The Queen inquires, “So what is the plan to get Darlene under control?” Lizzes replies, “I take that you’re aware of what happened.” The Queen confirms, “Yes, she almost killed someone?” Lizzes admits, “I don’t have a plan, but I have an idea.” The Queen agrees, “Good, let’s get it done sooner rather than later.” Lizzes concedes, “Ok, Your Majesty, no disrespect, but talking about Darlene makes us mentally exhausted. Can we please talk about something else?” The King bursts into laughter and remarks, “You created this problem, but now you’re having second thoughts. It’s too late. She’s all your problem.” Lizzes says, “Excuse me,” and rises from her seat. She then declares, “I lost my appetite. I’m going to bed.” The Queen is now looking at the King with a disgusted expression. The King defensively responds, “What?!! It’s the truth.”

CHAPTER 45

HARD HEAD MAKES A SOFT ASS

That next morning, Lizzes leaves the palace before breakfast to meet Darlene at the coffee shop. To Lizzes' surprise, Darlene is already there. Lizzes walks in, and they hug each other. Lizzes inquires, "So, how do you feel?" Darlene responds, "Better than ever." Lizzes explains, "So the reason I wanted to talk to you is that I want to move you, your family, and my coworker's family into Greater Landing. It's safer there, and you will be protected by the guardsmen." Before Darlene can answer, Prince Edward walks in. He makes his way over to Lizzes and Darlene as everyone watches him.

He approaches Lizzes and Darlene's table and greets them, "Good morning, ladies." Lizzes replies, "Good morning," but Darlene senses something isn't right with Prince Edward. Lizzes notices Darlene's intense gaze as she says, "Good morning," without blinking. Lizzes addresses him, "Prince Edward." Darlene looks at Lizzes and asks, “He’s a Prince?” Lizzes confirms, “Yes!” Darlene relaxes a little, but she can tell something is up with Prince Williamson. Lizzes offers, “Would you like to sit down?” Prince Edward accepts, “Sure, thank you,” and continues, “So, you’re Lizzes? I’ve heard a lot about you from the Prince on what you have accomplished. I don’t know it all, but I can see certain things, like the transformation of Greater Landing. It’s amazing what you’re doing with that town.” Lizzes responds, “Well, thank you, but what did you really stop by to say?”

Prince Edward now realizes he’s not dealing with an ordinary woman. He admits, “Well, since you put it that way. I am curious about how a 5’4, 115-pound woman can compete with grown men? I’m not completely sold on that.” Lizzes warns, “Prince, it’s best that you keep your words to a bare minimum. I know you’re a tall and big gentleman, but if I were you, I would just let it go.” The Prince clarifies, “I mean no disrespect, but I just can’t see what I’ve been hearing. I just can’t.” Lizzes grows tired of Prince Edward’s sarcastic remarks. So, she challenges, “Would you like a demonstration?” Prince Edward questions, “With whom?” Lizzes answers, “You!” Prince Edward reacts, “You’re kidding, right? I’m 6’8 inches, and I weigh 275 pounds. You can’t be serious.”

Lizzes turns to Darlene, “Would you like to give the Prince a little Demonstration?” Darlene responds, “I thought you would never ask,” and then gets up to walk outside. The people in the coffee shop now turn their attention outside. Lizzes gestures, “After you, Prince.” The Prince stands up with a smile on his face and walks outside. He comments to Darlene, “That’s a pretty dress. Are you sure you want to mess it up?” Darlene replies, “No, I don’t,” Just then, she activates the suit! As Prince Edward watches, he takes a step back and is stunned! Lizzes instructs Darlene, “No weapons!” Darlene acknowledges with a nod. The Prince is unsure about what to do. He heard about the suits but had never seen one in action. One of Lizzes’ guardsmen walks up to Prince Edward and advises, “I wouldn’t test her if I were you.” But Prince Edward is cocky and declares, “I must find out what all the talking is about Darlene.”

He begins circling Darlene. The guardsmen also activate their suits just in case Darlene gets out of control. Darlene wraps herself up with the cape. The Prince stops, puzzled by what has just occurred. But he continues to move behind Darlene and attacks her. He tries to grab Darlene around her throat, but Prince Edward doesn’t know that she can see him through the built-in mirrors at eye level on the side of her hood. As Prince Edward reaches out, Darlene spins around quickly, grabs his arm, and literally throws him about 8 feet into the air and 25 feet away. He lands on his right shoulder and breaks it in several places.

The guardsmen and Lizzes rush to the Prince’s aid as he screams in pain. One of the guardsmen assists the Prince’s injury by popping his shoulder back in place, which slightly eases the pain.

Lizzes orders, “Pick him up and take him to the hospital.” Lizzes approaches Darlene, who has deactivated her suit. She questions, “Did you have to throw him that far and injure him like that?” By shaking her head, Darlene responds, “He needed to learn a lesson. His pride and ego needed to be broken. Don’t worry. It could have been worse.” One of the guardsmen walks up to Lizzes and states, “This is his own fault. We tried to stop him. You can’t blame Darlene for this one.” Lizzes instructs the guardsmen to escort Darlene home and informs Darlene, “You will be moving into Greater Landing starting tomorrow.”

Lizzes directs one of the guardsmen to inform Prince Edward’s parents of the incident. Lizzes now is wondering how the Queen and King are going to react to another incident involving Darlene within two days. Upon entering the palace, Lizzes finds the King and Queen in the study having coffee after breakfast. As she enters the study, both the Queen and King know something is wrong by the look on Lizzes face. The Queen demands, “What is it now?” Lizzes reports, “There has been an accident with Prince Edward.” She assures, “He’s fine. He just has a broken collarbone.” The King inquires, “How did he get a broken collarbone? Did he fall or something?” Lizzes clarifies, “Yes, he fell, with a little help from Darlene.” The Queen exclaims, “My goodness, what did she do this time?”

Lizzes defends, "It wasn't her fault, Your Majesty. Prince Edward wanted to test her abilities, and he wouldn't take no for an answer. So, there was a little demonstration that involved Darlene throwing him about 8 feet in the air and 25 feet away. He landed on his shoulder and broke his collarbone." The Queen remarks, "Even though he brought it on himself, Darlene didn't have to injure him. There are a lot of maneuvers she could have done to prove her point." She declares, "That's it!" She summons four of her palace guardsmen and orders, "Tomorrow morning, remove Darlene from her home and bring her and her family here. She's too dangerous to be in the public eye. Leave their belongings. Just bring their clothes and personal items. They can live in the south wing of the palace." Then she shouts at Lizzes, "She is your problem! So you go and tell her the news!" Lizzes accepts, "Yes, Your Majesty, I will after lunch." The Queen demands, "No! Now! Turn around and walk your pretty little self out that door, and do it now!!!"

Lizzes responds, "Yes, your majesty." Lizzes is now nervous because she hasn't seen the Queen this angry in a long time. Earl, the Princess, and the Prince hear the Queen screaming and immediately come running into her study. The Prince inquires, "Is everything ok?" Lizzes assures, "Everything is fine. I will be back shortly," and walks out with her guardsmen. Earl is puzzled, so he walks after Lizzes to find out what's going on. He calls out, "Lizzes! Stop!" She turns around, clearly upset. Earl asks, "What happened?"

Lizzes explains, “Oh, Darlene broke Prince Edward’s collarbone.” Earl says, “What!!?” Lizzes replies, “I’ll tell you when I get back. Right now, I have to go talk to Darlene.” Earl says, “Okay,” and returns to the Queen’s study.

The Queen has already informed the Princess and the Prince of what happened, and they are actually not surprised. The Prince remarks, “Well, I told Edward not to try anything, and he wouldn’t listen, so it’s his own fault.” The Queen agrees, “I agree, but Darlene is dangerous to the public and needs to be watched at all times. So, she will be living here.” Earl reacts, “What?!! Darlene will be living here?” The Queen confirms, “Yes, so make her feel at home when she gets here tomorrow.” Earl acknowledges, “Yes, Your Majesty,” and departs. The Princess confides to the Queen, “You know, Earl is scared of Darlene to death.”

CHAPTER 46

NOT FOR THE FAINT OF HEART

Lizzes leaves the palace with her seven guardsmen heading back to Darlene's house. On her way, she stops at the hospital and walks into Prince Edward. He is leaving the hospital with his parents and his arm in a sling. Prince Edward's parents, the Duchess and Duke of Kent, confront Lizzes, "Are you responsible for this?" Before Lizzes can respond, Prince Edward interjects, "No! She's not responsible. I am. It's my own fault. I was told what not to do, and I did it anyway. Please, do not blame her." Lizzes remarks, "I just stopped by to make sure you were ok."

Prince Edward assures, "I'm ok. My pride is a little hurt, but I'm ok." Lizzes offers, "When you are healed, come see me. I have a job opportunity for you." Prince Edward reacts, "Really?" Lizzes confirms, "Yes." Prince Edward commits, "I will do that. Thank you." Lizzes exits the hospital and makes her way to Darlene's house. When she reaches Darlene's house, she finds Darlene sitting on the porch, enjoying a cup of coffee. Lizzes steps out of her carriage and walks to Darlene's porch. She takes a seat, and Darlene probes, "Ok, what's wrong? You have a worried look on your face." Lizzes reveals, "Well, the Queen wants you and your family to come live in the palace. She thinks you're a danger to the public." Darlene looks at Lizzes and responds firmly, "You tell the Queen that I respectfully decline her offer." Lizzes corrects, "It isn't an offer. It is a demand." Darlene insists, "Well, tell the Queen that I respectfully decline her demand. Tell her I am not a danger to the public unless the public puts me in danger. Other than that, I'm perfectly fine."

Lizzes looks at Darlene and declares, "I'm not going to tell her that. I'm just going to tell her that you agreed to move into Greater Landing instead of the palace." Darlene asserts, "Do what you must, but I will not be living in that palace." Lizzes responds, "Ok. I have another task for you. I need you to locate 13 women who would like to be trained and become the lioness guardsmen." Darlene questions, "Lioness guardsmen? What kind of name is that? And what for?" Lizzes explains, "They will be my own personal female security, and you will be in charge of them." Darlene inquires, "Will they undergo the Royal Guardsmen training?" Lizzes clarifies, "No! You will be the only female with that training. They will go through our new martial arts training for six months. As you will also go through it."

She continues, "After six months of everyday training, you will be given a special suit that will be completed in a couple of months. Plus, I have a surprise gift for you and the 13 women that you find soon." Darlene questions, "What type of women are you looking for?" Lizzes specifies, "Hard-working woman with an edge. Like you." She adds, "There need to be three blacks, three Asians, three Hispanic, two whites, and two Indians. Can you do this for me?" Darlene agrees, "Sure, I can, but when do you want this done?" Lizzes responds, "Three days." Darlene exclaims, "Three days!!!??" Lizzes confirms, "Yes. Can you do it?" Darlene looks at Lizzes for about ten seconds before remarking, "My goodness, you and your ideas! Ok, I will do it." Lizzes concludes, "Good, can you start now? While your kids are in school."

Darlene looks at Lizzes shakes her head, and says, "Ok, but I'm going to need a horse." Lizzes confusingly replies, "A horse?" Darlene confirms, "Yes, a horse. The type of woman you want are hard-working farm women. They are athletic and in shape. And I know exactly where to get them from." Lizzes questions, "Where?" Darlene responds, "The Women's boot camp prison is 10 miles out in the country." Lizzes reacts, "Wait a minute, prisoners?!" Darlene assures, "Yes, they will be perfect." Lizzes expresses concern, "Darlene, I don't know about that. I was thinking more like ladies who have regular jobs in the cities." Darlene asserts, "Hey, you said I would be in charge, so let me be in charge. Or you can get someone else to do it." Lizzes agrees, "Ok." Darlene advises, "Relax! Show some trust!"

Lizzes instructs one of the guardsmen to give Darlene his horse. Darlene requests, "I need a signed letter from you giving me jurisdiction over the prison for the next four days." Lizzes directs the guardsmen to bring her a jurisdiction letter from her briefcase. Lizzes signs two letters. She instructs, "Give one of these to the warden." Darlene acknowledges, "Ok." She activates the suit! Lizzes protests, "Hey, wait! What are you doing? You don't need to activate your suit for this!" Darlene counters, "You must be crazy if I'm going to ride 10 miles to a prison and show up in a dress. Who's going to respect me with a dress on?" Lizzes thinks for a second, then says, "Darlene, promise me you won't hurt anyone." Darlene responds, "No, I can't promise you that! I'll be back before my kids get out of school," and then she rides off. One of Lizzes' guardsmen asks, "Should we follow her?" Lizzes states, "Yes, but take the southeast route, so she won't see you coming. Don't interfere unless you have to." Another guardsman suggests, "Wait until they see her with a brown caped hood and mask on. They are going to be scared to death."

Lizzes murmurs, "I don't feel so good. Take me to the martial arts training facility." A guardsman hands Lizzes some water, and they proceed towards the training facility. Upon arrival, she enters the facility and observes the 14 Panthers guardsmen, the venomous

20, and the 12 righteous ones engaged in separate training sessions. Lizzes gets a big smile on her face as she sits down at a table to observe. As she is watching, one of the Panther cubs sleeping with the other cubs wakes up, sees Lizzes, and approaches her. Lizzes picks up the cub and glances at its name tag.

The name tag says Michael. The cub takes a big yawn and begins to fall asleep. Lizzes cradles the cub close to her chest, and it falls asleep. Then, she gently rubs the cub while it sleeps in her arms. Lizzes gets a glance from everyone, but they continue to train. Meanwhile, Darlene has reached the outskirts of the women's prison forest. As she passes through the forest, she hears cries of, "Please stop, don't touch me, no!" Darlene jumps off the horse and climbs into the trees to get a better view. She positions herself two stories high in the trees. What she sees angers her!!! She witnesses three of the prison's male security guards forcing themselves on three young women.

One of the men slaps the young woman he's assaulting, causing her to fall to the ground. The other men do the same, causing the other two young women also to collapse on the ground. Having seen enough, Darlene leaps from the tree, landing just above the three women's heads. As she lands, dust blows into everyone's face. The three men, down on their knees, trying to take off the women's clothes, raise their eyes to look at Darlene. They get off the ground really fast and back away even quicker as they pull their guns.

Darlene helps the three women to their feet and inquires to them, "Are you alright?" The women respond, "Yes."

Darlene instructs them, "Go stand behind that tree." The ladies gather themselves and move behind the tree. As they take cover, Darlene overhears them whispering, "That's a woman." The three men, not sure of what to expect, also realize that it's a woman. They shout at Darlene, "Hey, who are you, and what are you doing here?" Darlene replies, "I'm here on official business, and it looks like I just showed up on time." One of the men asserts, "Look bitch, I don't know who you are and why you dressed up in that suit with that long-hooded cape and mask on, but you have about five seconds to reveal and surrender yourself for interfering with prison officials' disciplinary business." Darlene takes five steps forward and remarks, "That was five steps and five seconds. Now what?" They are now ten feet away from each other. The three exchange concerned looks. One of the men yells, "Fire!!!" Darlene spins and drops to the ground, her cape shielding her. The bullets begin to bounce off Darlene's cape. Knowing she could kill the men very easily, but instead, she jumps about ten feet in the air, taps both shoulders and activates her weapons system.

She then taps herself on both hands, and they fill up with hard rock sand. As she's coming down, she spins in the air and throws the sand at the men. The sand instantly triples in volume, blinding their vision. Darlene lands with one knee down, and the other up, with the cape fully wrapped around her. With blinding speed, she rushes them. She delivers a round-house kick to one, uppercuts another, and punches the last one, knocking all three men out. After the cloud of hard sand dissipates, the three men are lying there, knocked out. Darlene taps her forearms, activating the ropes weapon system, causing ropes to come out of each sleeve under her control.

She begins to tie the men up. She then places all three men on their horses. The three women are watching this as Darlene lifts these men with one arm. After placing the men on their horses, she calls to the women, "You can come out now." The three approach Darlene, kneel before her and begin to pray to her. Darlene steps back and exclaims, "Hey, please get up. I'm no God!" The Three women get up and Darlene deactivates the suit. She explains, "See, I'm just a woman just like you. But I'm a trained fighter." One woman asks, "How did you beat those three men?" Darlene reactivates the suit, causing the women to jump back.

Darlene responds, "I will tell you later." She then questions, "How long have the prison security guards been raping you, ladies?" One of the women reveals, "I've been here for three years, and I've been raped several times a week." The other women confirm the same experiences. One of the ladies adds, "They rape everyone that's in good shape and has a nice body." Darlene commands, "Take me to the warden. Grab the horses with the men on it and follow me." Darlene mounts her horse. While riding to the prison, she observes many women harvesting vegetables in the fields. All types: collard greens, turnips, cabbage, kale, okra, eggplants, tomatoes, cantaloupe, watermelon. Darlene is very impressed by the farm. She muses, “So this is where most of the vegetables come from.”

Darlene asks the women, “What are your names?” The black lady replies, “Melody.” The two white ladies say, “Samantha, but everyone calls me Sam.” Another white lady says, “I’m Sunny.” She queries further, “All those workers, prisoners?” Sunny explains, “The ones on the right side that are fenced in are prisoners. The ones on the left without fences are paid workers.” Darlene asks, “Who do they work for?” Sunny replies, “Two brothers named Jeff and John Dweet.” Darlene exclaims, looking at Sunny, “You’ve got to be freaking kidding me!” Sunny elaborates, “They are former prisoners who couldn’t get a job in the cities, so the Dweet brothers hire them to work this side of the farm which they own.” She continues, “They get paid pretty well, but it’s very hard work.” Darlene inquires, “Those are some really nice farmhouses on the left side. Who lives there?” Sunny informs, “All the paid workers. That’s where we are trying to go when we get out in a year.”

Darlene has other plans for them, but they just don’t know it yet. As they pass the farm and walk four more blocks, they come face to face with ten prison guards who have been watching Darlene and the ladies coming from a distance. The guards are on the other side of the gate. Upon seeing Darlene and their fellow security guards tied up, they point their guns at them. One security guard demands, "Who are you, and why are my men tied up?" Darlene asserts, "My name is Darlene, and I'm a Female Royal Guardsman." The Security guards scoff, "Royal Guardsman!!" and burst into laughter! Darlene instructs the ladies, "Go stand behind that brick building." While the ladies go behind the building, Darlene gets off her horse. The security guard, who must be the chief of security, retorts, "Everyone knows there are no female guardsmen. Take that hooded cape off and show yourself, and let my men go!"

Darlene mutters to herself as she walks towards the gate with her jurisdiction papers, "I just can't get any damn respect." The security guards command the three women to come out from behind the brick building and return to the prison. He questions, "How did you get outside the gate anyway?" As the ladies walk from behind the building. Darlene shouts to the ladies, "Stay where you are!!" The ladies move back where they are. As Darlene walks towards the gate, she yells at the security guard, "You know exactly why these ladies are outside the gate!! Those three men were trying to rape those ladies outside of the fence. That's why they're tied up, and that's why the ladies are outside of the gate!" She reaches the gate and hands the security guard the jurisdiction papers. Darlene states, "Take that to your warden." The security guard reads it and sees the Duchess of Sussex's seal and signature.

He looks at Darlene and then at his guards. He turns back at Darlene and rips the jurisdiction form up. He declares, "This letter is a fake!! You have three seconds to reveal yourself and tell me who you really are!!" Darlene backs up! She's pissed! Guns are pointed at her. She spins, kneels down, and activates her suit's weapons. As she wraps her up in the cape, she declares, "I tried the correct way! Now, let me try the wrong way!" She leaps twenty feet into the air, spinning. As she spins, she taps her biceps and activates her steel four-inch spears. The security guards are so shocked to see what they're seeing that they forget to fire their guns. She fires around two hundred steel spears at all ten security guards. Landing on the other side of the fence, she watches as the guards fall to the ground, temporarily paralyzed. Darlene looks back and warns, "I'll deal with you when I get back." She grabs three guardsmen's guns and throws them to the three ladies. Darlene asks, "Do you know how to use these?" Sunny confirms, "Yes!" Darlene replies, "Good! Watch the gate, and don't let anyone in." As she enters the prison, one of the three ladies, Melody, exclaims, "Holy shit!!!!"

CHAPTER 47

A BOMB INSIDE THE WOMEN'S PRISON

D**arlene** enters the prison and hears voices and footsteps echoing from around the corner hallway. She activates the sand weapons. Her hands fill up with hot, moist, vaporized sand. This time, she slowly blows the sand from her hands. A sand cloud begins to fill all the hallways on the first floor as she is constantly blowing it out of both hands. She can now hear men's voices saying, "I can't see. The sand is in my eyes. Get out, get out. I can't breathe." Darlene now positions herself by the corner hallway. As the men come towards the gate trying to escape, she attacks them.

Darlene can see perfectly as the sand cloud parts around her. She takes out twenty-two men on the first floor. After tying them up and tossing them outside, she heads to the second floor, where the warden's office is located.

Outside, the two guardsmen show up to the prison forest and enter through. Both guardsmen notice the area where Darlene and the three men fought. They find bullets and lots of sand. So, they knew Darlene was there. They activate their blue suits. As they enter the prison farm grounds, they see everyone on the left has stopped working and now has made their way to the prison gate. Approximately fifty women and twenty men are gathered. The female prisoners on the right side have also stopped working and make their way to where Darlene is stacking security guards. As the two guardsmen approach, the crowd parts to allow them through. They stop at the gate.

The three ladies have guns pointed at them. The ladies notice that the guardsmen's suits are just like Darlene's, but in a different color. One of the guardsmen reassures the ladies, "Relax, ladies, we are Royal guardsmen, just in a different uniform." Melody asks, "Are you friends of Darlene's?" The guardsman confirms, "Yes, we are. What happened here?" Sunny explains as she lowers her gun, and the other two ladies follow her, "These three men here on the horses tried to rape us again in the forest, but Darlene stopped them. These ten men here disrespected Darlene by ripping up the jurisdiction papers she tried to show them."

She adds, "Those twenty-two men, and counting, are the ones she's fighting now and throwing them out as she catches them." One guardsman inquires, "So I take it that these prison guards have been raping and physically assaulting you women for a long time?" Melody confirms, "Yes! It happens every day." The two guardsmen exchange wrathful glances. One remarks, "Let her finish. We will just wait here until she's done." Suddenly, the door opens, and Darlene throws out seven more. She notices the guardsmen watching her and gives them a stare. They give her the guardsmen go-ahead signal. She acknowledges it and goes back inside. One of the guardsmen asks Melody, "How many security guards are working at this prison?"

Melody responds, "Thirty-five in the daytime and about 15 at night." She informs, "A lot of women also get assaulted and raped at night. The second shift will be showing up in about an hour." The guardsmen declare, "And we will be waiting." Just then, out of the side door, eighty young women come running out. They gather at the front gate, in front of all the men Darlene has taken out of the prison. Moments later, from the second-floor side windows, the warden's three personal security guards are thrown out headfirst, believed to be dead or at least hurt really badly. Then Darlene comes out with the warden tied up, and she's pissed!!

She yells at him, "These women are not your personal sex slaves! These are human beings, not animals you keep in a cage. For your crimes at this prison, you and your men will be taken to London and handed over to the city police." Then Darlene goes over to check on the men she threw out the window, and they are still alive. Darlene instructs six women to take those three men to the prison doctors. They grab the three men and take them away. All the ladies are screaming with joy! She then walks up to the ten men, temporarily paralyzed. She points her arm at the steel needles embedded in the men, retracting them back into her sleeve and reloading them into the weapons chamber. As Darlene unties their feet, the ten men begin to regain sensations of their bodies. She instructs four more women to bring the four transport carriages and load the men inside. Once the men are loaded, Darlene asks the guardsmen if they would transport the men back to the city police?

The guardsmen agree to transport the men back to the city after the second shift security guards arrive in about 15 minutes. Darlene asks, "There are 15 more guards?" The guardsmen confirm, "According to Melody, there are." Darlene acknowledges, "Ok." She orders all the women to return to the prison and initiates a lockdown. The guardsman informs, "We will leave the men in the transport carriage on the side of the road for them to see as they make their way towards the front gate where we will be waiting." Darlene directs, "I need everyone to take a shower who needs it and remain in your cells with the cell doors open as we prepare ourselves for what's to come." They are all talking about Darlene and how she defeated all of the security guards.

Melody exclaims, "You should have seen her in the forest." Darlene goes outside and joins the guardsmen. Instead of the ladies going to take a shower and into their cell, they all find a window to look out of in anticipation of what's about to happen. Darlene and the two guardsmen are now waiting outside the gate. One of the guardsmen notices the women peering out from the windows. He comments, "So much for lockdown." Darlene questions, "What?!!" The guardsmen point towards the upper windows. Darlene turns, shakes her head, and says, "Let them look. They deserve to see what's about to happen to these rapists and women beaters!!" Just then the second shift security guards break through the forest. As they approach, they see no prisoners in the fields. They make their way towards the gate and see their co-workers in the transport carriages along with the warden. They can't talk cause Darlene has taped their mouths. They can only gesture with their head and feet's movement. The security guards stop!

Two of them get off their horses and try to unlock the door to let them out. But their co-workers are trying to tell them no and to ride away. However, they don't get what they're trying to say. The two security guards are hit with Darlene's steel darts and are temporarily paralyzed and fall to the ground. Their horses get agitated and start jumping on their front legs. The remaining thirteen guards see three horses riding towards them. They pull out their guns and start shooting. The guardsmen and Darlene are about a hundred yards away; they leap in the air off their horses about fifty feet up and seventy-five yards forward. They land fifteen feet in front of the security guards and wrap up in their cape. The bullets are bouncing off of them. The thirteenth security guards see this and try to ride away, scared to death, not knowing what they are fighting against. As they turn, they are struck by paralyzing hot steel darts from a guardsman, causing them to tumble from their horses. The two guardsmen tie the men up and then retrieve their hot steel darts.

While all this is going on, Darlene is staring at the guards in the transport carts with her hand guns popping in and out of the bottom of her sleeves. The security guards see this and are scared to death. One of the guardsmen notices Darlene doing this and yells her name, "Darlene!!" She turns towards the guardsmen and goes to help them in loading the security guards into the transport carts. Darlene instructs the guardsmen not to leave until she returns. She gets on her horse and rides back to the prison. She goes inside and directs the three ladies, "I need you to take these rifles and handguns, post up on the second floor, and shoot anything that comes this way. I'll be back tomorrow morning." She orders all the women to go to their cells and lock themselves in. Darlene leaves and assists the guardsmen in transporting the security guards to the city police.

Milton Keynes UK
Ingram Content Group UK Ltd.
UKHW041427141124
2855UKWH00034B/116